VANISHING ACT

Also by Seth Jacob Margolis

False Faces

VANISHING ACT

SETH JACOB
MARGOLIS

ST. MARTIN'S PRESS
NEW YORK

Design by Dawn Niles

Library of Congress Cataloging-in-Publication Data

Margolis, Seth Jacob.
Vanishing act / Seth Margolis.
p. cm.
"A Thomas Dunne book."
ISBN 0-312-08770-5
I. Title.
PS3563.A652V3 1993
813'.54—dc20 92-41158
CIP

First edition: March 1993

10 9 8 7 6 5 4 3 2 1

For Laurie, Jane, Dan, and Kate

ONE

Joe DiGregorio tripped over a body submerged in the whirlpool at the New York Health Club, but that wasn't really the most extraordinary thing to happen to him on the second Tuesday in April.

It began with a phone call to his office, which was shoehorned into one corner of Alison's not-very-large-to-begin-with living room. He'd moved in with Alison nearly six months ago.

"Investigations," he remembered to say into the phone.

"This Joe DiGregorio?"

He affirmed that it was, omitting to add that friends called him Joe D. The caller sounded anything but friendly.

"Can you meet me in half an hour?" The voice was deep and authoritative, with that slightly impatient edge that often signified a person used to having his requests obeyed.

Joe D. looked down at his calendar, which was virginal except for a Saturday morning bar mitzvah of a second cousin of Alison's in three weeks. "Who is this?"

"That doesn't matter. You want a job?"

"I need to know who I'm working for."

"Forget it, then. I'll call Discrete Investigations, right after you in the yellow pages. Right after DiGregorio."

Joe D. weighed his annoyance against his desperation for a job. Desperation was heavier. "Okay, but what kind of job are we talking about?"

"Ten-thirty, southwest corner of Seventh Avenue and Thirty-sixth. Wear a Yankees hat so I'll know you."

"I'm a Mets fan."

"What I'm paying you, you'll learn to love the Yankees. Ten-thirty."

Joe D. checked his watch. It was, indeed, 10:00. He'd have to take a cab to the garment district, probably a six dollar ride from Alison's place—no, from *their* place on the Upper East Side. That six dollars would put him solidly in the red for the week—business wasn't exactly booming. What was the opposite of booming? Joe D. wondered, as he debated whether to meet Mr. X in half an hour. Busting? Deflating? Slumping? He tried this last one out: Business was slumping. No, that implied that it had once been booming.

Actually, business was comatose.

His only work since leaving the Waterside police force consisted of a few small employee theft cases he'd handled for Alison's father and a few of his rag-trade cronies. They left him feeling more indebted to Alison than before, despite the fact that they enabled him to contribute his share of the mortgage and maintenance for a couple of months.

"Don't worry, darling. Things will pick up. Every new business takes a while to catch on."

"Yours didn't."

"That's different," she had said with an equivocating shrug, and neither had been anxious to continue the conversation. Alison had been laid off by Bloomingdale's during the bankruptcy, and had decided to pursue a long-held dream of owning her own store. She'd borrowed money from her father and opened Many Fetes, about the same time Joe D. moved in. Alison's years as a buyer paid off. She had a knack, apparently, for choosing exactly the right mix of clothes for women like her: Hardworking professionals in their thirties who liked to dress up once in a while and didn't mind paying through the teeth for the privilege. The only bad part of her success was that she worked six days a week from morning till night. Perhaps if Joe D. hadn't been so underworked it wouldn't have bothered him, but he found himself bored and restless, and had to resist the urge to stop by the shop eight times a day, offering his services as stock boy or gofer or whatever.

He missed Alison too, some days, even after six months of living together. Sometimes just the sight of her after even a brief absence caused him to catch his breath. She was beautiful, which partly explained this, but she also had a very changeable face—she never looked exactly the same to him twice. "It's my nose," she'd once explained to him.

"Your nose?"

"Charlie Firestein threw a softball at it in the third grade. Deliberately."

"Unprovoked?" Joe D. had said with mock horror.

"Completely unprovoked. And the worst thing was, when the school nurse wrote her report, she said that I'd stepped in the path of a flying ball. It still makes me crazy to think about it."

"Ever thought of taking a contract out on Charlie Firestone?"

"Fire*stein.* Very funny. Anyway, my nose wasn't broken, but it grew kind of funny after that."

"Doesn't look funny to me."

"From the left, it looks straight." She turned to the left to show it off. "But from the right it kind of bows out, with a bump." She showed him her right side. "Every time I see my right profile I think of Charlie Firestein and that nurse's report and I still feel angry."

Joe D. thought she should be grateful to Charlie Firestein, for he had helped provide Alison with a face that no man could ever grow tired of, in his humble opinion. Her penchant for harboring grudges, on the other hand, was a less attractive if equally salient quality.

Joe D. felt uneasy about the mysterious phone call, but he couldn't muster any excuses for not keeping the appointment, and if Alison found out he'd turned down a job she'd hit the ceiling. It was Alison who had urged him to open his own agency, and now he could sense her impatience with his progress. It wasn't just the money. It was the fact that he worked out of her—no, *their* apartment. It was the way he lingered in bed in the morning, rousing himself only to kiss her good-bye as she left for the store at eight. It was the sense of hopelessness that he couldn't conceal at the end of a long, vacant day, waiting for the phone to ring in an apartment in which he still didn't feel comfortable, in a city that still didn't, probably never would, feel like home. Only Alison, his feelings for her, felt totally right to him.

Joe D. got out of the cab at Times Square and found a tourist shop on Forty-third Street. He bought a Yankees cap for $2.95, bringing his investment in this case to over nine dollars. He walked the rest of the way to Thirty-sixth Street and then waited on the southwest corner for someone to make his day.

Standing still on the corner of Seventh Avenue and Thirty-sixth Street is a lot like trying to tread water in a grade-three rapids. After being broadsided by several irate pedestrians he took shelter behind a mailbox. At 10:30 precisely a black limousine the size of his childhood home pulled up. A back door opened and Joe D., sensing that he was making the biggest mistake of his life, got in.

It was like entering a dark cave, except that the limo was all soft edges, plush. The man sitting next to Joe D. was soft too, with copious jowls and pink, puffy hands dusted with dark liver spots. He was wearing large sunglasses and was facing away from Joe D., as if to shield his identity. The driver was invisible to them, thanks to a darkly tinted screen over the front seat; Joe D. took it on faith that there *was* a driver as the car smoothly left the curb and headed downtown.

"I'm prepared to offer you fifty thousand dollars for what I have in mind," the man began.

"Maybe we should introduce ourselves," Joe D. said in an effort to retain some control of the situation. Outside, he could see people on the sidewalks gawking at the tumescent limo, but he knew they couldn't see him behind the tinted glass. Oddly, this made him feel more vulnerable, more at the mercy of the man sitting next to him.

"I know who you are, and you needn't know who I am," the man said with perfect composure, as if this was self-evident. He was still facing away from Joe D. "Are you interested?"

"Fifty grand is fascinating. What's the job?"

The man shifted in his seat, practically squirmed, as if he were proposing an especially devilish prank.

"I want you to kill me."

TWO

Later, at his health club, Joe D. rehashed that limo ride as he plied the Nautilus machines and other, equally convoluted devices designed to work even those tiny, obscure muscles with no discernable practical purpose.

"Kill you? I hardly know you," Joe D. had replied with what he thought was an appropriate level of flippancy. But the man was serious. Dead serious, Joe D. was tempted to think.

"Of course I don't intend to actually *die,"* the man said. "It will only appear as if I've been killed."

"An insurance scam," Joe D. offered.

"I have no life insurance. I'm too rich for life insurance."

"Then why?"

"Yours, Mr. DiGregorio, is not to reason why."

"Yeah, mine is but to do and die. If you want me to, uh, kill you, you better at least have the courtesy to tell me why." Actually, Joe D. had no intention of taking this guy up on his offer, but he was undeniably intrigued.

The man turned contemplative for a few moments as the car sped down Seventh Avenue, gliding across potholes with cushioned scorn. He was still facing away from Joe D., shielding his identity. "I'll tell you this much. I am in love with someone with whom I intend to spend the rest of my life. I also have a wife. The latter will think I've been killed, while I live out my days with the former. I have more than enough stashed away to live more than comfortably."

"Divorce might be simpler."

"Not for me. When I die, my company will pass into a trust, the proceeds of which will benefit my wife, and one or two others, during their lifetimes. If I divorce my wife, she'll ask for half of my wealth. I think she'll have a good case. If she wins, the company will have to be sold or dismembered in order to pay her. I couldn't stand to see this happen. I have no children, Mr. DiGregorio. Only my business."

"But you're willing to walk away from it. . . ."

"That won't be easy. But every morning I can pick up the *Wall Street Journal* and reassure myself that it is still running smoothly in my absence. Part of the pleasure of raising children, I understand, is watching them become independent."

"How do you intend to kill yourself?"

"I don't intend to kill myself. I intend for you to do it."

"Then how?"

"I didn't accumulate nearly a billion dollars by giving things away for nothing. Are you in or aren't you?"

Joe D. was thinking about the nearly-a-billion-dollars part. A billion dollars.

"Are you in or aren't you?"

"I investigate fraud. I don't commit it."

"Seventy-five thousand then."

"You just told me you're a billionaire. Do you think I'd settle for seventy-five thousand?"

"How much, then?"

"Forget it. I'm not interested at any price."

"One million dollars." A slight desperation was evident in his voice.

Joe D. hesitated. A sum like that demanded a certain respect. A million dollars would put him in the black for quite awhile. Maybe forever. It killed him that he wasn't even tempted. "Sorry."

The man sank back into his seat. "I'll find someone to do it, you know."

Joe D. had no doubts on this score.

"You're a fool, Mr. DiGregorio. You're a fool to turn down more money for a few days' work than you're likely to earn in a lifetime."

"It's against the law to . . ."

"Fuck the law," the man exploded. He started to turn to Joe D. but restrained himself. His right hand clenched and unclenched on his right knee. "The law is for union members and civil libertarians and welfare mothers. People with real power, people like me—for us the law is irrelevant."

He said this without irony or bitterness, as if it were self-evident. "People like you?"

"Men with wealth and power beyond your imagining. Men who got that way because they weren't imbecilic enough to turn down a million dollars for a few days' work." He rapped on the window behind the driver, and the limo pulled over and stopped. "This is where you get off," he said, still not looking at Joe D. He appeared to be breathing heavily after the tirade.

Joe D. got out and squinted in the late-morning sun. The limo already seemed like another world, a climate-controlled land of soft edges and absurd propositions. He made a point of memorizing the license plate number. Disappointingly, it was a z-plate, a daily rental.

Joe D. changed into a bathing suit and headed for the Jacuzzi, his way of appeasing his body after putting it through motions it had never been designed to execute. Despite the exercise, he felt keyed up, on edge. It was turning down all that money that was doing it. A million tax-free dollars would take a lot of pressure off him. A lot of pressure off Alison too, who, after all, was footing both their bills. The money thing was a big issue between them; like a hyperactive child, it tended to disrupt more than a few of their meals and spoil many an otherwise peaceful weekend.

It was the body in the Jacuzzi that finally managed to distract him from the events of that morning. The club was quiet that afternoon—only one person was in the adjacent swimming pool—and Joe D. had the whirlpool to himself, or so he thought. He stepped slowly into the scalding water, which took some getting used to. Gingerly he made his way across it to an underwater bench. But after just two steps his right foot came down on something that was definitely not concrete. It gave under his foot in a way that made his stomach lurch. He hesitated for just a moment, then plunged his arms into the churning, opaque water and pulled up, with some effort, the limp, puckered body of an elderly man.

Finding the body had at least rescued him from an idle afternoon in Alison's. . . . in *their* apartment, waiting for the phone to ring. He'd shaken awake the lifeguard and stood by while he went through the motions of resuscitating the dead man. Then he'd waited for the police to arrive, then someone from the coroner's office, who said it looked like a heart attack. "You jump into the Jacuzzi from the cold swimming pool, you take your chances," he said matter-of-factly. "I've seen half a dozen of these cases."

Joe D. didn't think he'd be using the Jacuzzi anytime soon. In fact, as he left the club at 7:30 that evening, he thought he might take up jogging, which was Alison's favorite pastime. It was cheaper, for one thing (joining the club had been a splurge to begin with) and the chances of stepping on a body were very slight, as long as you avoided certain parts of Central Park.

THREE

The next day, Wednesday, Joe D. called a former colleague on the Waterside police and persuaded him to trace the license plate of the limo. Joe D. had made it to lieutenant before resigning last fall to join Alison in New York. The Linda Levinson case had put him off police work, anyway, though it had had one positive result: He'd met Alison Rosen the previous summer, while investigating the homicide on Fire Island. It took some mental gymnastics to savor a new relationship while blacking out the circumstances under which it had begun. The Linda Levinson case had been Joe D.'s first homicide, and though he'd been praised for his work on it, he didn't really think you could call a case successfully resolved when virtually all the suspects, innocent or not, ended up dead.

He'd taken a lot of heat, quitting the Waterside force. Though Waterside was only an hour east of New York City, moving to Manhattan was viewed as the equivalent of moving to Beirut, only New York was more expensive. And giving up a secure, practically tenured spot on the Waterside police force was seen as the financial equivalent of investing your life savings in S&L stock. He hadn't bothered explaining that he was in love, nor that the Linda Levinson case had soured him forever on being a Waterside cop, perhaps on Waterside itself.

At least he still had a friend or two on the force he could call on for the occasional favor. It took less than an hour, but the news wasn't worth even that wait. The limo had been rented from King David Limousine Service, and when Joe D. stopped by their offices on Amsterdam Avenue, he was told by someone who was probably not the King that it had been rented, for cash. Joe D. managed to contact the driver that afternoon, who said he never even got a look at the man. "I pulled up to the corner of Seventh and Forty-fourth, like I was told. Before I could get out this guy jumps in and shoves five hundred bucks through the window, tells me to head downtown, pick up a guy on Thirty-sixth. That was you, right? Then you get out downtown and he tells me to keep driving. Coupla minutes later, we hit a red light and he jumps out, not a word to me, just like that."

Case closed, Joe D. thought, feeling relieved. He'd been uneasy walking away from this fraud in the making but figured he'd done all he could to prevent it.

Alison's hours were so long, and Joe D.'s cooking skills were so underdeveloped, that most nights they ordered something in. Chinese, chicken, burgers, you name it—in Manhattan, you could always find someone to bring anything to your apartment as long as you were prepared to pay extra for it. In Long Island, you were pretty much stuck with pizza, unless you were willing to get in your car.

Tonight they ordered in from the appropriately named Jackson Hole, which specialized in burgers as large as a Rocky Mountain. Joe D. told Alison about the limo service.

"I guess you'll have to wait and see if any billionaires die in the next couple of weeks."

Joe D. had thought of this. That morning he had read the obituaries in the *Times.* No billionaires today, just a former ambassador to someplace in Africa, a vice president of Merrill Lynch, a writer of off-off-Broadway plays, an actor, (both of the latter from AIDS), and six columns of paid death announcements of people who'd led lives deemed unfit to print by the *Times.* "Maybe I should have gone along with the guy, just till it got hairy. I mean, he gave the limo driver five hundred dollars, he would have given me ten times that just for starters, just for playing along."

"Forget it, Joe D. That's not the kind of business you want."

"I'm getting desperate."

"Something will come up." She said this with so little conviction that they both resumed their assaults on their burgers, which they'd abandoned only minutes ago, rather than pursue the topic of Joe D.'s fading prospects.

After dinner Joe D. went for a walk. He invited Alison, but she said she was exhausted. Joe D. was never exhausted these days; it was the major occupational hazard of idleness.

Fortunately, the city offered innumerable pleasures for the insomniac stroller. Back in Waterside, no one walked much farther than the distance from their front door to their car. But New York was a city of walkers—even overweight women had good legs in Manhattan, he'd noticed. Joe D. liked to leave Alison's apartment on Seventy-third Street and head towards the East River. Tonight he followed his usual route, entering Carl Shurz Park at Seventy-ninth and walking along the river up to Gracie Mansion. (The first time he'd made this walk, with Alison, she'd told him that her grandmother had been delighted when Abe Beame was elected mayor, replacing John Lindsay. "Thank God there's finally a Jew in Gracie's Mansion.") He left the park at Ninety-second and headed over to Third Avenue, which was invariably busy, something he liked in a city street. Then he walked back to Alison's . . . *their* apartment.

"Where'd you go?" Alison asked, as she always did.

"To Gracie's," he answered, as he always did.

Alison was already in bed, reading a magazine. Joe D. undressed and joined her.

"I was thinking . . ." he began.

She put down the magazine. "Uh oh."

"Maybe I should think about the city police. Nothing's happening, and I'm getting tired of waiting. Besides, the pay's good."

"The pay's *okay,"* Alison corrected him. "But what kind of future is there in being a cop? At least with your own business . . ."

"I don't have a business. I have myself and a phone. *Your* phone."

"And some clients."

"Clients referred by your father."

"That's how you get started in business, through referrals."

Joe D. turned away from her. He wished that Alison wasn't so caught up in his having his own "business." It just wasn't so important to him what he did for a living, as long as he was active and earning money. It had always been like that for him. But Alison took working very seriously, and now that she had her own store she was almost fanatical. He suspected that her real motivation in urging him to stick it out was that she didn't want to be living with, and perhaps eventually married to, a mere cop. The president of a private investigations agency, on the other hand, particularly one that specialized in corporate work, would suit her much better.

"Look, Joe D.," she said, and put a warm hand on his shoulder. "Maybe I push too hard. You must think I'm some kind of Lady Macbeth. And maybe it is important to me that you're successful. I know that's what you think."

He turned around, impressed, as he often was, by her insight into his feelings.

"Just give it until the end of the year, okay? See what happens. If nothing develops, okay, then you can start exploring alternatives."

"Like the city police force."

Alison rolled her eyes. "Even that." She picked up her magazine, then put it down.

They made love before turning out the lights. Sex for them was the balm that soothed all wounds. It was the one part of their relationship that they could both lose themselves in. Alison could immerse herself in her work, and Joe D. could find relief from pressure (or, worse, the total absence of it) at the gym or walking the streets of Manhattan. Only sex was a shared release.

Alison fell asleep in his arms within seconds, but Joe D. felt himself growing less drowsy by the moment. Should have run today, he thought. He carefully extricated himself from under Alison and slipped out of bed. He checked the digital clock. Midnight. He put on a bathrobe and walked into the living room, closing the door quietly behind him.

He placed a CD on the player, Bach's *Goldberg Variations.* They had been written for an insomniac, and though they never produced anything but bliss in Joe D.—a heightened alertness, if anything—he figured he'd give it a shot. He kept the volume low and lay down on the floor to listen. The recording was by Glenn Gould on the piano. Joe D. had a harpsichord version too, but thought the piano would be more soothing, despite the eery moaning of the pianist that wafted up now and then behind the glorious music. He tried to picture Goldberg attempting to sleep while a paid musician picked away at a keyboard across the room. He thought about men who paid other men to do for them what they should be able to do for themselves: Put them to sleep, put them to "death." Money was power, not just over other people but over oneself. With enough money you could be lulled to sleep by heavenly music even before the phonograph had been invented. With enough money you could discard one life like an out-of-fashion suit and put on another, or so one very rich person believed. And without money, Joe D. knew firsthand, you were not only stuck with the life you led, you felt powerless to even change its direction.

Or so he felt on a bad day.

He woke, hours later, to a dull thud not far from his ears. He opened his eyes and could tell from the muted, unfamiliar light edging in from the corners of the blinds that it was very early in the morning. He stood, stretched for a moment to work out the kinks, then looked around for the source of the thud. Nothing in the apartment seemed out of order. He checked the clock on the oven in the kitchen. 5:30. Then he figured it out. He returned to the living room and opened the front door. There, on the floor, was the source of the thud: Thursday's *New York Times.*

"Alison, are you awake?"

She was now.

"I know who it was."

"Who who was?" she said groggily.

"The guy who asked me to kill him."

She propped herself up on her elbows.

"It's on the front page of the *Times.* George Samson. He was murdered. It's got to be him."

Alison looked at him and nodded dumbly. "What time is it?"

"Five-thirty. Almost six," he added encouragingly.

"I'm going back to sleep."

She rolled over and appeared to do just that. He made a pot of coffee and studied the obit. A few minutes later, wearing a flannel robe, she joined Joe D. in the living room. She took a big swig from Joe D.'s coffee mug and asked him how he knew it was the same guy.

"I don't know for sure. But the article says he's one of the richest men in the city. He has a wife and no kids."

"Picture?"

"Yeah, but I didn't get a good enough look at him the other day. It *could* be him, though."

"Let me see."

He handed Alison the front section. "Jesus," was all she said after reading for a few moments.

It *was* horrible. George Samson, founder of Samson Stores, had been found shot dead with a single bullet in the face alone in the back of a taxi. The driver, Salik Mafouz, who'd arrived in New York from Pakistan just six months ago, had also been killed with one bullet. The cab was discovered on an abandoned pier next to the West Side Highway. Samson's wallet was found next to him on the back seat, all the money gone. Police were labeling the case a "hijacking," the latest in a series of such robberies in which a thief jumps into a vehicle stopped at a light, orders the occupant to drive to a secluded spot, and then picks him or her clean. The only difference in this case: The passenger and the driver had been killed.

"George Samson, I can't believe it."

Alison said this with such conviction, Joe D. thought she must have known the man. "You knew him?"

"Of course I didn't know him. But I heard of him."

"Oh."

"You never heard of George Samson?"

Joe D. shook his head, admitting to the failing.

"Samson Stores?"

"Never shopped there, no."

"They're women's stores, Joe D. About a thousand of them, I'd guess. All over the place. Samson's one of the richest men in America."

"So he led me to believe, assuming it was him."

"Are you going to tell the police about what happened the other day?"

"Not until I can prove that it was Samson I met with. Anyway, if he was going to fake his death, he'd make sure there wasn't a body left over to ID. This sounds like a genuine murder."

Alison got up and poured herself a cup of coffee. "God, George Samson killed in the back of a cab. It seems so . . . common."

"A limo would have been classier?"

"Infinitely. Speaking of which, why wasn't he in his limo?"

"It was a rental, remember?"

"Yeah, but a guy like Samson must have a fleet of cars."

"Then he made a big mistake, taking a cab."

FOUR

"George Samson was a brilliant and innovative businessman, a loving husband, a devoted uncle, and, speaking personally, a warm and loyal friend."

These lines were delivered in a flat, fill-in-the-blanks voice by Seymour Franklin, once Samson's second-in-command and now his chief eulogizer (as well as chief executive officer of his company).

Joe D. sat in the last row of the filled-to-capacity room, the largest chapel in the poshest funeral parlor on the Upper East Side (or so Alison had told him). If he'd had anything better to do he wouldn't be here. And just about anything would be better than this amazingly dry-eyed funeral.

Joe D. didn't know what he was expecting to learn at the funeral, or what, for that matter, was in it for him, as they say. Still, he couldn't stay away.

The eulogy was interminable. George Samson was a tycoon, a visionary, a philanthropist, a saint. Joe D. knew that it was considered bad taste to bring up the faults of the deceased at his own funeral, but he hadn't heard so many superlatives since Schwarzkopf's final press briefing in Saudi Arabia. Wasn't it customary to include little quips about the deceased's idiosyncracies, delightfully embarrassing recollections that would make him seem more human, and thus all the more likable?

But no humorous anecdotes were forthcoming from Seymour Franklin, and so George Samson failed utterly to come to life after his death for the thousand or so "mourners" gathered to pay their last respects.

After the service the crowd didn't so much disband as form discrete groupings. Factions was the word that sprang to Joe D.'s mind, for each group appeared to turn its back, literally, on the others. One faction swarmed around Seymour Franklin, congratulating him on his eulogy. Lots of handshaking in this faction. Another faction hovered about an astonishingly thin, taut-faced woman in a short black dress whom Joe D. guessed was the widow. Still another faction flitted about a woman who looked to be in her early thirties. She, too, was dressed in black, though her punky hair and coolly bored expression suggested that black was her favored color even when she wasn't attending funerals. The smallest faction consisted of perhaps a dozen, mostly elderly men and women. The men wore yarmulkes. They appeared no more distraught at Samson's demise than any of the others, but as they peered out of their tightly formed group they seemed to be casting disapproving glances at their fellow mourners. A final faction swarmed about no one in particular, but seemed reluctant to leave, preferring instead to ogle the other three factions.

Joe D. didn't belong in any group and was about to leave when the prospect of yet another long, empty day persuaded him to return to the chapel for a little of what Alison had once referred to, in what turned out to be the trigger for a minor argument, as "practice development." He stood in the back of the large room and surveyed the four factions before choosing to prospect in the largest, that of Seymour Franklin.

It wasn't easy making his way through the tightly knit crowd: No one was willing to cede a favored position close to the new CEO of Samson Stores. Joe D. eventually managed to fight his way to the epicenter of this group, as dense with accumulated power as an atomic particle. When he tapped Seymour Franklin on the shoulder he half-expected to receive an electrical shock. Instead he received an automatic smile followed by a look of aloof indignation. "Do I know you?" Franklin said with more feeling that he'd revealed in the entire eulogy.

"Here's my card, Mr. Franklin," Joe D. said as softly as he could. He waited while Samson glanced at it.

"Investigations?"

"In case you're not satisfied with what the police tell you," Joe D. said.

Samson seemed about to hand the card back to Joe D. but pocketed it instead. Then he turned away from Joe D. as if from a waiter offering unwanted hors d'oeuvres.

Central Park was at its springtime best that afternoon. Magnolias and cherry trees were in bloom, forming a pastel border around the reservoir jogging track. Joe D. circled the reservoir once—nearly one-and-a-half miles—then circled it again, and, inspired by the bracing April air and wondrous foliage, he circled it again. Four-and-a-half miles is not a prudent distance for a first-time jogger. Joe D. knew he'd suffer tomorrow. No pain, no gain, he thought. He'd always hated that expression.

The message light on Alison's answering machine was blinking when he returned. He figured it was Alison, and decided to take a shower before unlocking its secrets. Hope beat out despair and he changed his mind. "Mr. DiGregorio," began a female voice. "This is Seymour Franklin's office.

Would you kindly call Mr. Franklin at your earliest convenience." She gave a phone number and hung up.

Joe D. returned the call at his earliest convenience, which happened to be right away.

"Is there something about George Samson's death you know that the police don't?" Franklin said by way of greeting after his secretary had put Joe D. through.

"Possibly," Joe D. replied honestly.

A long pause. "How soon can you be in my office?"

Franklin's office overlooking Fifth Avenue was the length of a bowling alley and about as cozy. Crossing from the door to Samson's massive desk seemed to take forever—or at least, it took long enough for Joe D. to consider and reconsider exactly what he was doing there. Second thoughts were something of a specialty of his. Franklin nodded at a chair in front of his desk without offering his hand.

"Now, what is it you know?"

Joe D. decided his best strategy was keeping what he knew to himself. "Hold on, Mr. Franklin. Why don't you begin by telling me why you called me."

Franklin took a deep breath and let it out slowly. "The police, as you know, are labeling Samson's death a 'hijacking.' A random thing. I have my doubts."

"What kind of doubts?"

"Samson was at a board meeting of the New York Art Alliance Tuesday evening. The meeting began at seven and ended about nine-thirty. His chauffeur had the night off, so he took a cab home. The killer could have waited outside the Alliance's offices on West Sixty-fifth Street, followed Samson, jumped into the cab at a red light . . ."

"Whoa. How could the killer have followed a moving cab? Unless we're talking about an Olympic sprinter, which would narrow the list of suspects."

Samson grimaced at this attempt at humor. "I know who killed him," he said evenly.

"Have you told the police?"

Franklin shook his head. "I have no proof. That's why I called you. You can get the proof I need. Then I'll go to the police." Easy as pie, he might have added.

Joe D. felt the tips of his fingers begin to tingle. A job! "Who's your suspect?"

"Mona Samson." The words escaped his mouth like a belch. "The widow."

"And the motive?"

"Money," he said, as if this were obvious. "Theirs was not exactly a close marriage. Now she's one of the wealthiest women in New York. And single."

"Does she have a lover?"

"I wouldn't know. I don't move in the Samsons' social set. George and I were colleagues but hardly friends."

"But in the eulogy . . ."

"My last professional chore for George."

"And now you run the show here."

"Correct."

"So Samson's death wasn't exactly tragic for you either."

Franklin seemed about the respond to this but stopped himself. "Do you want this job, Mr. DiGregorio, or not?"

"My fees are three hundred dollars a day plus expenses."

Samson nodded readily and Joe D. instantly wished he'd mentioned a higher sum. "I'll have my secretary draw up a check for the first week. I believe you fellows like the first week in advance?"

Joe D. assured him that this was the case.

"Who identified the body?" he then asked.

"Mona," Franklin replied. "I understand George was a bit of a mess. The shot was point-blank in his face."

Which could make positive identification a problem. "Did they check dental records?"

"What for? Mona knew her husband, with or without his face on."

"Tell me about Samson," Joe D. asked.

Franklin thought for a bit before answering. His eyes narrowed and his lips puckered slightly; apparently talking about his late employer was painful.

"Whenever I hear people talk about a workaholic, I think, You don't know the meaning of the word unless you've met George Samson. He was the most driven man I ever knew. For the eighteen years I knew him, he arrived in his office every day before anyone else, and left long after the cleaning crews arrived. Never took a day off, not even for vacations. If he wasn't here he was visiting stores. He used to bring me along sometimes. His pace was exhausting, and he was several years older than me. Cheap as he was, he bought a jet a few years ago so he could visit even more stores in less time. I thought the jet would make traveling easier. It didn't. With the jet he just doubled the number of stores we'd visit. Sometimes we'd see ten stores in a day, in ten different cities. And then we'd have dinner in a motel in some god-awful town and all George would talk about was the goddamn business. Not politics, sports, women, nothing but the business. And the next day? Ten more stores."

"Sounds like your life will be easier, now."

"If that's an insinuation . . ."

"Call it a conclusion."

"Well, it will be easier, then. Not that I'm one to slough off. But I don't own half of this place. George pushed himself in a way that only an owner would. He had eight hundred and ninety locations, and he treated each of them as if they were his first and only store. In some ways I don't think he ever stopped thinking of himself as Georgie Samowitz of the Lower East Side."

"Samowitz?"

"Sure, he changed his name. His father owned a hosiery store on Orchard Street. I think it was called Samowitz's, maybe Samowitz Hosiery. The family lived around the corner. George and his sister used to work every spare minute in the store. His mother, too. But it never went anywhere. They never starved, but they weren't too far away from poverty, either. George would never talk about those days, but you hear things in this business. He went to work at the store full-time after the war. He had big plans for it. His father thought he should go to college, maybe afterwards to law school or medical school. He was an immigrant and dreamed of his son making a life for himself beyond Orchard Street. I guess George had dreams too, but they involved the store, not college."

Franklin stopped and asked Joe D. if he wanted coffee. He declined. Franklin pressed a button on his phone and said "coffee" into the speaker. Nothing else, just "coffee." Joe D. was eager to hear how Georgie Samowitz had ended up one of the wealthiest men in America—he always had a soft spot for rags-to-riches stories (who didn't?)—but Franklin seemed disinclined to continue without coffee. Joe D. shifted in his chair, waiting. Finally, after an uncomfortably silent interval, a secretary, suitably attractive, brought Franklin's coffee in a china cup and saucer on a small silver tray. No Styrofoam in the Samson Stores executive suite. It was a long way from Orchard Street.

Franklin took a sip and resumed his story. "George had big plans for the store. He wanted to enlarge it, expand the assortment, maybe open a branch uptown. His father was happy just to make the rent each month. Samowitz Senior wasn't exactly a powerhouse, from what I hear. I think George lasted about two years in the business. It was George's mother who ruled the roost, and when push came to shove she sided with her husband. George's big plans were thwarted. So he left the business and opened his own store on Fourteenth Street. He called it Samson's, not Samowitz, and eventually he changed his own name too. I don't think he ever spoke to his parents or his sister again. George was like that. Cross him once and you're finished. He didn't have an ounce of forgiveness in him."

"Any of them still around?"

"His father died a few years after the split. His mother died about ten years ago. George didn't tell me any of this. His secretary gossiped with my girl. Apparently George had her send a check to pay for the funerals but didn't attend himself. What a hard-ass."

"And the sister?"

"I'm not sure. There's a gaggle of relatives out in Brooklyn somewhere. Second cousins, great aunts and uncles. No one too close. Orthodox, some of them."

Joe D. recalled the gang of somber, mostly elderly men and women at the funeral.

"So Samson opened his first store on Fourteenth Street. . . ."

"That's right. Turns out he had a genius for merchandising. This was right after the war. George guessed that young women were tired of shortages and drab colors. He filled his shop with knockoffs of the latest styles from the department stores uptown. Bright colors, bright displays, everything upbeat. Pretty soon he outgrew that first store. He opened a second one on Forty-second Street. Then he opened one in Harlem. I think he branched out into the suburbs in the early fifties. Before long he was on the main street of every city in America. Always the same merchandise, the same displays. Everything standardized."

Joe D. pictured Samson Stores spreading across the country the way the old newsreels showed Hitler's army spreading across Europe.

"Then, in the early sixties, he made the decision that put him in the major leagues." Franklin paused to take a sip of coffee from the delicate china cup. "Shopping malls were opening up everywhere. Some of his competitors saw them as a threat, and put money into modernizing their downtown locations. Samson saw them as an opportunity and started opening stores in every new mall that came along. If he was short of cash to finance the new locations he'd close a downtown store rather than miss out on a new shopping center.

Some of his competitors went out of business in the sixties. Samson flourished. He signed thirty-year leases in some of these malls that are worth millions today."

"When did you join the company?"

"Around that time, in the sixties. The company was already well on its way. But I was able to give it some structure, impose some controls. George was brilliant at spotting good locations and filling the stores with the right merchandise. But he had absolutely no interest in finance or accounting. When he tried to go public in the early sixties the investment bankers told him he'd have to hire a number-two man to oversee operations. I'd already developed a good reputation in the business so George brought me on board. I don't think he ever liked the idea of a second-in-command. He thought he could do it all himself, and he knew that I was considered his successor. He didn't think of himself as mortal, I suppose."

No, Joe D. agreed, Samson thought he could mastermind his own death just as he'd masterminded the growth of his empire.

"George had no friends, not even in the business. And he was ruthless. I once saw him physically attack a manufacturer who wouldn't cut his prices during the '82 recession."

"Samson attacked him?"

"He had summoned the man to his office to talk over terms. The guy owned a big blouse company. He'd been giving the buyers a hard time over prices. Samson didn't even let him into his office. As soon as his secretary announced him he raced out into the waiting area and started screaming at the guy: 'You son of a bitch,' he yelled. 'After all the fucking business I've given you over the years.' 'But George,' this poor schnook says, 'we cut our prices any more, we're losing money on the deal.' That's when George went at him. Started pushing him on the chest, had the guy backing out into the outside hallway. 'I don't want to hear your fucking problems,' he yelled. I heard the commotion and went to see what was happening. I held George back but he kept on yelling. The manufacturer left in a hurry, I can tell you."

"Sounds like quite a guy."

"George? He was a genius. That manufacturer, he calls the next day and drops his prices ten percent. During that recession, a lot of our suppliers went out of business. Happens a lot on Seventh Avenue during a slump. But Samson Stores? Record profits every quarter."

"Any of his suppliers mad enough to kill him?"

"Sure, dozens of them. But business has been good these last five, ten years. If he'd been killed after the '82 recession, then I might have suspected one of our manufacturers. But lately George was a hero on Seventh Avenue. No, if you're looking for his killer, look no further than his wife."

"When did she enter the picture?"

"About fifteen years ago. George had never married, though he went through a lot of gorgeous women. I wonder what they saw in him?" Franklin rolled his eyes to underscore that this was a joke. "But he never got serious. The only thing he cared about was his company. Then he met Mona."

Joe D. recalled her from the funeral. Attractive, in a gaunt way, but hardly *gorgeous.* "What made Samson fall for her?"

"That's a question I've been asking myself for years. You ask me, she's repulsive. No meat on her. No *tits.* Not in the same league as his other dates, though she was younger then. I think what George saw in Mona was his ticket to respectability. No matter how rich he got, he was still a peddler of polyester in the eyes of a lot of the high society types in this town. A Jewboy from the Lower East Side. Mona showed him how to spend his money in the right places, the places where it would do him some good. And Christ, could she spend it. Their apartment alone cost six million, and probably twice that to decorate, with all the Picassos and Monets and who knows what. But it got written up in all the right magazines, so I suppose it was worth it. And every time he bought a painting he made news. Always paid top dollar. Not that I've ever been to his place. To Mona, I was a reminder of the grubby way George made his money. She wanted no part of me or Samson Stores. Except the dividends, of course. Mona liked the dividends. She was the one, by the way, that moved us into these offices. Before Mona came along we were on two floors of an un-air-conditioned building on Seventh Avenue. Where we belong, as far as I'm concerned."

Joe D. didn't buy this. Franklin looked very much at home in these posh digs, and Joe D. doubted he'd be moving the company back to the West Side any time soon. "You said they didn't have a close marriage. . . ."

Franklin shrugged. "I'd see them at charity dinners now and then. They looked like colleagues more than husband and wife. Which, in a sense, is what they were. He married her for her social skills. She married him for his cash. It was a merger more than a marriage. If George ever mentioned her it was only to complain about her spending."

"I'll pay her a visit tomorrow."

"Good. Now, tell me what it is you know about George Samson's death."

"Nothing more than I read in the paper," he said smoothly, then grinned, as if proud that his "practice development" ploy at the funeral had paid off. Joe D. had only one advantage going into this case: A strong hunch that the victim had wanted to arrange his disappearance before he disappeared for real two days ago. He resolved not to second-guess his initial decision to keep this bit of information to himself.

Alison was elated that Joe D. had a new client. She offered to buy him dinner to celebrate, but he insisted on taking her out. He picked her up at Many Fetes, and they walked to their favorite pasta place where the tiny chairs were murder on the coccyx but the food was balm for the soul.

She lifted a glass of white wine. "Things are going to be great from now on."

Joe D. knew what she meant by *things.* His lack of an

income was putting a strain not just on their finances but on their relationship as well.

They talked constantly about the need to separate what they felt about each other from practical considerations, like work and the mortgage (or Alison talked constantly about this—Joe D. had limited patience for such conversations, while Alison relished them, it seemed). But they never could compartmentalize their lives, and so a kind of cold war had settled between them, with the threat of open hostilities just an ill-chosen word away. Until tonight.

"If it wasn't a random burglary, then it had to be someone Samson knew," Joe D. said, thinking aloud.

"Why are you so sure?"

"If it was random, a hijacking, then the perp just waited at a certain corner for a cab or a car to stop at the light. But if the murderer had Samson in mind, he couldn't just wait at a certain corner and then hope that the light would be red. What are the odds of that? He'd have to know Samson's route that night, wait for him somewhere along the route, and then flag him over—whether or not the light was red."

"And Samson wouldn't tell the cable to pull over unless it was someone he knew."

"Right."

They concentrated on their pastas for a while. Growing up, Joe D. had thought pasta meant spaghetti and linguini, plus ravioli from a can. Since moving to Manhattan, he'd been introduced to *capellini, rotini, penne,* fresh ravioli stuffed with lobster, *fussili,* and a host of other pastas he never could quite remember.

"Thing is, I still don't have any proof that Samson was the guy I met with."

"But it does seem coincidental, this guy getting murdered the day after he hires you to fake his death."

"Did you ever have any dealings with Samson Stores, or know anyone who worked there?"

She shook her head. "They're down-market from Bloomingdale's I don't think I ever knew anyone who worked for them. They cater to teenagers and women in their twenties who want the latest trends but don't have a lot of cash. They're in all the malls. They're incredibly profitable."

"I talked to Samson's successor today. Apparently the old guy wasn't too popular."

"He's a legend. There's a Samson wing at the Met, a Samson dormitory at NYU *and* Columbia, a Samson Library at Lincoln Center."

"Generous guy."

"He's got a lot left over."

They walked home slowly, relishing the cool evening air. When you're feeling low, New York is the worst place in the world to be, its smart stores and smartly dressed inhabitants a constant reproach. But when you're feeling good, New York is a city of limitless possibilities, a treasure house of pleasures just waiting for your selection.

Tonight, holding Alison's hand, Joe D. felt great, and New York seemed like heaven.

FIVE

The Samson apartment was on Fifth Avenue in the seventies. Even Joe D., who was only just learning what was and wasn't a "good" address in Manhattan, knew that Fifth Avenue in the seventies was prime real estate. The building occupied an entire block front on Fifth, but the lobby was unexpectedly small, even intimate. The floor was highly polished white marble with little black-marble inserts. There was a fireplace at one end with a seating area in front of it. The lobby in Alison's—*their* building—was much larger, but the Samson's lobby reeked of money seasoned by class, while their lobby reeked only of the former.

A uniformed doorman opened the gleaming, smudge-free brass door for him. Another man, also in uniform, announced him over the house phone. A third man took him up in the elevator: Apparently, automatic elevators were a modern convenience but not a modern luxury.

Joe D. stepped off the elevator on the eleventh floor

expecting the usual apartment-house corridor of doors. Instead, he found himself in a rectangular vestibule girded with polished-wood wainscoting and lit by a large crystal chandelier. The floor was an expanse of luminous pink marble. There was only one door, and it was opened even before he rang the doorbell by a white maid in a black uniform.

"Mrs. Samson is expecting you in the library," she said almost shyly, looking at the floor. Did she know he was a private investigator?

She led him through another hallway ("foyer" is what such rooms are probably called, Joe D. thought), this one filled with oil paintings that looked vaguely familiar. In a less expensive place they'd be posters of museum pictures. Here they were no doubt the genuine article; even with virtually no knowledge of art he thought he recognized a Picasso, a Degas. They entered a library through an oversized door. Once Joe D. was in the room his escort retreated, closing the door behind her.

The room was enormous in every dimension—width, length, height—and lined with floor-to-ceiling bookshelves. Joe D. guessed that the leather-bound books were the buy-them-by-the-yard type. Two oversized couches were positioned before a massive, immaculate fireplace. On one of these was perched a woman so thin, so insubstantial, she barely made an impression in the puffy upholstery. In fact, the library itself seemed to overwhelm her; in this dignified, carefully composed room, she struck Joe D. as far less consequential than one of the several table lamps scattered throughout the room, or one of the doubtless unread leather books.

"I still don't understand why my husband's murder isn't being handled by the police," she said, once Joe D. had introduced himself and sat across from her. Unlike Mona Samson, he felt himself engulfed by the sofa, swallowed.

"They are investigating the murder. But Seymour Franklin felt . . ."

"Frankly I'm surprised that Seymour hired you. If this

wasn't a random murder, then I'd say he's your prime suspect."

"Franklin?"

"He's the new C-E-O." She over-enunciated the three letters with a sarcastic twang, as if she were describing the new leader of a Boy Scout troop. "It's what he's always wanted."

She was perfectly composed, bordering on smug. Joe D. decided to shake her up. "He seemed to think that you had the best motive."

"My husband's money?" she said with an amused grin. It would take more than a murder accusation to rattle her. "I had more than I needed when George was alive. No, Seymour wants to muddy the waters because he knows that once I'm in charge of Samson Stores I'll have him fired."

She smiled, relishing the thought, but her skin was as taut as a filled balloon—a very narrow balloon; she managed only a stifled grimace. Her hair was pulled straight back from her face and clenched in a tight little knot at the back of her head, giving her a wide-eyed, perpetually startled expression. With all the surgical work (even Joe D. could tell that this was a much-altered face), it was difficult to gauge her age, which was doubtless her intention. Joe D. guessed she was somewhere in her forties.

"Seymour Franklin is a parasite. An overpaid parasite. He knows I have no use for him."

Joe D. searched for some evidence of grief on Mona Samson's face. He found none, and wondered if her face was capable of expressing grief. Perhaps her tear ducts had been surgically removed. Her voice, a breathy, unaccented monotone, seemed ill-suited to expressing any emotion stronger than benign amusement.

"But if the company makes money, what do you care who runs it?"

"When George's will is probated I'll *own* Samson Stores. Or, I should say, the seventy-five percent of the shares formerly owned by my husband. The public owns the rest." She made *public* sound like a remote and ill-understood species.

"As long as you bring up the will . . ."

"I get everything," she said matter-of-factly. "The shares, the real estate, all this." She raised two long, bony arms to encompass the room and countless others like it. Then, after a long pause in which she seemed to be stewing over something, she said: "And George's niece, Joanna Freeling. There's been an accommodation for her."

"Accommodation?"

"A million shares of Samson Stores. Worth about thirty-two million at yesterday's close."

Some accommodation. "She was close to her uncle, I take it."

"She was his only living relative other than some . . . people out in Brooklyn. George never saw them. Joanna's mother was George's sister. Both parents died some time ago. I'll give you her address before you leave. You might want to talk to her."

"Why would I want to do that?"

"I assume Seymour has you on a daily retainer. So you might as well stretch it out as much as possible. I have no doubt that when you're through you'll find that poor George was simply at the wrong place at the wrong time."

"That reminds me—how many people knew he was going to be at the Art Alliance meeting the night he was killed?"

She hesitated before answering. Joe D. found it difficult to watch her—she was like a well-dressed anatomy chart, all bones and ill-disguised veins—so he glanced behind her and caught a glimpse of Central Park and the West Side through a window.

"I knew. And the other members of the board knew, of course. George's secretary, Felicia Ravensworth, knew. No one else that I can think of."

"You're sure?"

"Check with Felicia. She'll know." Like her late husband—or, at any rate, like the man in the limo with Joe D.—Mona issued commands easily. Delegating was perhaps her chief talent. That and dieting.

"Is Wednesday the regular day off for your chauffeur?"

"We have no set schedule. He worked during the day and then George must have given him the night off."

"May I speak with him?"

Instead of answering, she pressed a small button hidden among a variety of no-doubt precious items on a table next to the sofa. Porcelain figurines, an ashtray, two obelisks, a tiny marble bust on a bronze stake attached to a Lucite stand. Whatnots, his mother would call them. Alison would call them *tchotchkes.* Mona Samson probably called them objets d'art.

A few moments later the door to the library opened and the maid reappeared.

"Serena, could you ask Tony to step in here?" Mona Samson said without turning to face her employee. He was almost surprised that her voice carried across the large room, given the insubstantiality of her body.

Tony Manganino was a heavyset man in his early forties. He had gray hair and a thick, unruly gray moustache. He wore a wide blue tie that he hadn't managed to pull up all the way. He looked uncomfortable in the tie, and even more ill at ease in the Samson library.

"I already told the police," he said in a tough, New Yawk accent with a defensive edge. "I dropped Mr. Samson off at the Art Alliance at six and he gave me the rest of the night off. I garaged the car, had a few drinks at McGlade's—that's on First in the eighties—then I came back here. Ask the others," he added unnecessarily.

"Did he often give you the night off like that when he was out?" Joe D. asked.

"Once in a while. The other night, he said he didn't know how long he was going to be. Said he'd take a cab."

Such benevolence didn't jive with what Joe D. had heard

about George Samson. Perhaps he had a soft spot for his driver. "How long did you work for Mr. Samson?"

" 'Bout a year."

"And before you?"

Manganino shrugged. "There was another guy. He didn't last six months, and the guy before him . . ." He looked nervously at Mona and stopped himself.

"Anything else, Mr. DiGregorio?" asked Mona testily.

Joe D. shook his head and thanked Manganino, who turned and left.

"Well," Mona said, clasping her hands on her imploded lap, as if signaling that the interview must be drawing to a close. "I think that's about all I have for you."

Joe D. swallowed and asked the question he'd been holding back. "Did your husband have a lover, Mrs. Samson?"

He watched carefully for a reaction but detected none. "He had . . . flings. I don't know as I'd call any of them *lovers."*

"You knew about . . ."

"I knew only that he fooled around," she interrupted. "I wasn't interested in who they were or what they were."

"You don't think there was one in particular?"

She attempted a smile but succeeded only in squinting. "My husband had only one love. His company. There was no one in particular, as you put it. He cared for nothing but his company—not his employees, not his family, such as it was, not his customers. . . ." Here she broke off and seemed to laugh silently, as if the idea of her late husband caring for the legions of teenagers and working-class girls who'd made him rich was unbearably amusing.

"Are you sure there was no one special?"

"Positive," she said evenly. Then her hand again moved slowly but steadily to the buzzer, and Joe D. know his time was up. He fished for a card in his jacket pocket and handed it to her. "If anything comes up, here's how to reach me."

"Nothing will come up, I assure you. This was a random act of violence." After a moment's pause she added impassively, "a tragedy." She managed to locate a pen amidst the whatnots, *tchotchkes,* and objets d'art, and wrote something on the back of his card, which she returned to him. "Joanna Freeling, my husband's niece. That's her phone number."

The door opened.

"Please show Mr. DiGregorio out, Serena."

SIX

Joe D. left Mona Samson's building and headed east towards Lexington. There he caught the IRT down to Fifty-eighth, where he switched to the BMT out to Queens. Countless stops later he emerged somewhere in Flushing. He navigated streets crowded with Chinese, Puerto Ricans, and Pakistanis, until he managed to find the headquarters of the Apex Cab Company. He was an hour away from the Samson building by subway, but he might as well have traveled halfway round the world. The closest any of these people could get to the Samsons would be the front seat of a taxi.

Unfortunately for one former neighborhood resident, he'd come into contact with George Samson in just this way. Salik Mafouz had worked as a driver for Apex since arriving in America. He had a wife and three children back in Pakistan, waiting for Salik to send them enough money to join him in the promised land. Their wait had ended earlier this week.

Apex was located above a garage. Joe D. climbed a dark

stairway and entered a small, dingy reception area. A middle-aged man with at least two days' worth of stubble sat in a wire-mesh cage. He looked up at Joe D. and then looked back down. His plump fingers were sorting a huge wad of bills into neat piles of ones, fives, tens, and twenties.

Joe D. slipped a card into the cage. "I'd like to talk to someone about Salik Mafouz."

"So talk." He continued to sort bills.

"What I need to know is, did the driver fill out his route sheet for the Samson fare?" Most drivers who worked for a cab company, rather than owning their own licenses, were required to fill out forms indicating the origin and destination of each of their fares. Every New Yorker knew this.

"Cops already took the sheet."

Joe D. was not surprised. "Maybe you remember what it said."

The man actually stopped counting for a moment. "Nope, don't recall," he said at length, unconvincingly.

"You sure?"

The man kept on sorting, then said "nope" a second time.

Joe D. considered slipping a twenty under the mesh, but the huge pile of bills already there put him off. Still, he needed to know where Samson was heading after he left the Art Alliance. A hunch told him he wasn't going home, and that wherever he was going, he didn't want anyone to know about it. Why else dismiss the chauffeur on a night when he'd be needing transportation? Consideration had never been one of Samson's strong suits.

He decided, reluctantly, to send coals to Newcastle. "Think harder," he said, sliding a twenty under the mesh but keeping a finger on it.

The man eyed the twenty as if it were an obvious forgery. "Still can't quite recall."

Joe D. pulled the twenty back. "Too bad."

"Well, it wasn't completely filled out," the man said, as

Joe D. started to turn. Joe D. slid the twenty back under the mesh.

"Most drivers, they don't fill in the route sheets right away. Or maybe they just put the origin but not the destination. Fares don't like to wait. So the drivers wait until the first red light. Sometimes they wait till the ride's over. Sometimes they forget to fill them in at all, dumb fucks."

He looked to Joe D. as if to commiserate over the sad state of the cab driver's intellect. Joe D. wouldn't join in, so he continued.

"Mafouz, he filled in the origin all right, West Sixty-fifth. Even put the time, eleven-fifteen P.M. Cops liked that. But he never got to the destination, except for the first letter."

He paused, and Joe D. knew it would cost him. "What was the letter?"

"Well, that's just it. Most times, it's either an *E* or a *W*, right? As in east or west. And you know it's a street, not an avenue, since only streets have east and west before them, right? But if it's a number, then it's usually the address on an avenue, like Three forty-five Park Avenue."

"What was the letter?"

"For example, you see an *E*, you know it's a street on the East Side, even if the cabby never got to filling in the rest of the line. If it's a *W* . . ."

Joe D. shoved another twenty under the mesh. The dissertation ceased abruptly.

"G. The letter was *G.* Nothing else. Police figure he got a gun to his head before he could finish. First red light, probably, guy pulled a gun on him. Then took them over to the pier and shot 'em both. Blood all over the sheets and the meter. I know because I had to read them. Just because a guy's killed don't mean business comes to a halt. Believe me, our guys are shot at all the time. Well, not all the time, but you know what I mean. Though I gotta say, this was the first time a fare took it too. Christ."

* * *

Joe D. popped a tape into his Walkman and listed to Bach's second and third *Brandenburgs* on the subway back to Manhattan. The *Brandenburgs* were always a surefire antidote to the dreary, noisy subway. They exuded a vibrant enthusiasm, a self-satisfied but never smug cheeriness that he found irresistible, no matter what the circumstances. He briefly wondered what Bach would have thought of the notion of people listening to his music on tiny electronic cartridges while moving at forty miles an hour in underground tunnels. Then he decided he hated what-if meditations and concentrated on the music instead.

It was after four by the time Joe D. reached Manhattan. He figured he'd earned his three hundred dollars and could call it quits with a clear conscience. Instead of heading directly home he decided to stop in at the store to see Alison. He bought her a dozen yellow tulips on the way. One of the pleasures of New York, he was discovering, was the abundance of flowers for sale on virtually every block. Most of them were sold by Korean delis, but there were stores sprouting everywhere that carried nothing but roses.

Alison's store was nearly 1500 square feet, narrow and long. It was minimally decorated, with gray industrial carpet and white walls—the better to display the often florid merchandise.

Alison was helping a customer when he entered. The only other employee, a recent college graduate named Michelle, was behind the register in the front of the store.

"I can't get away with this," the customer was saying when Joe D. entered. Indeed, there ought to be a law, he thought, for the dress she had on was way too short for her over-ample legs. Alison, who hadn't noticed Joe D. entering, stepped back and squinted. Joe D. could see the opposing forces of honesty and greed waging war in her. Honesty won. "You're right. It doesn't do anything for you."

It makes an ass of you, Joe D. would have said.

"How about something not quite as . . ." Alison hesitated.

"Demeaning," Joe D. muttered, just loud enough for Alison, but not the customer, to hear. She turned, gave him a look, then smiled when he brought the tulips from behind his back. She turned back to her customer. "How about this," she said, and grabbed a more substantial dress in red satin.

The customer dutifully took the dress and headed for the changing room. Alison gave Joe D. a kiss and then frowned. "Now that you have some business you think you can come in here and chase away my customers."

"That dress could chase away an army."

"I've sold three of them already, at six hundred each."

"Jesus."

"How'd it go today?"

"Swell. I met with Mona Samson."

"You did? Gosh, if she started buying dresses here I'd be rich. Half the city follows her when it comes to fashion."

"They do? She looks like she'd have to shop in the children's department."

"She's a social X ray," Alison said, offhandedly.

"A what?"

"You know, from *Bonfire.*"

Joe D. was going to ask for a clarification when Alison turned her attention to her customer, who had reemerged wearing the red dress, which did indeed make a positive contribution to her appearance, disguising most of her excess flesh. Five minutes later Michelle was wrapping it up for her.

Alison stepped out with Joe D. for some air.

"You were great with her," Joe D. said.

"When you're paying the rent and overhead, you become a very persuasive salesperson. Anyway, she did find the right dress, which makes me happy."

"Make *me* happy and name all the streets in Manhattan beginning with the letter *G.*"

She thought for a moment. "Grand. Gansevoort. Gracie Square. Gerard."

"If you were George Samson, and you had a girlfriend, which of those streets would she live on?"

"Easy, Gracie Square. Gansevoort's in the Village—too bohemian. Grand's too Lower East Side for him. But Gracie Square's posh. If he had a girlfriend, that's where he'd keep her."

He walked back to the apartment with the tulips, which he placed in a vase. There were no messages on the answering machine, which didn't depress him as much as it did just a week ago. It was nice to be on a case. Then he called Joanna Freeling and introduced himself.

"But Uncle George was killed by a thief." Her voice could only be described as elegant, combining as it did a quiet confidence and a trace of arrogance.

He explained that he'd been asked by Seymour Franklin to confirm what the police already knew.

"I don't really see the point," she said. "But if my aunt's been telling you things about me, well, I suppose I ought to have my day in court as well." She laughed almost giddily and gave Joe D. her address.

On Grand Street.

SEVEN

Joanna Freeling lived in a loft building in the heart of Soho. Like the other structures on Grand Street, it was a former commercial building, six stories high with fire escapes running from top to bottom. Joe D. opened the front door and found Freeling's name on a small panel of buzzers. He buzzed her, then waited for an answer. He took in the general dinginess of the building, then buzzed again. He thought about why someone with $32 million would live in a place like this, then buzzed again. Finally, she answered.

"Who is it?" she said over the intercom, which managed to rinse her voice of its elegance. A moment later Joe D. was climbing three flights of the steepest stairs he'd ever encountered. They were metal and uncarpeted, and each step he took reverberated up and down the stairwell.

Joanna Freeling's door was open when he arrived.

"I could have brought the elevator down for you," she said. "It's manually operated."

"No problem," Joe D. panted.

She stepped aside to let him in. Now he understood why someone with $32 million would live here. And he understood why it had taken so long for her to answer. The loft was immense and obviously expensively decorated. Joe D. glanced around. An endless expanse of highly polished wood floor extended for acres in either direction, interrupted only occasionally by groupings of starkly modern furniture. On the walls hung gigantic paintings, the kind Joe D. often saw in galleries on outings to Soho with Alison on her rare breaks from the store, the kind that prompted him to wonder: Who would hang this in their living room? Who has the space? Now he knew.

"Wow," he said, after taking it all in. The loft seemed to demand a response.

"Thanks," Joanna said lightly, assuming the compliment. "I'm just finishing up a canvas. Do you mind if we talk in my studio?"

She led Joe D. toward one end of the loft. Sometime later they arrived in an area that wasn't as finished as the rest of the place, the floors splattered with paint, canvases leaning against the walls in stacks. Taped to one wall was a large canvas, perhaps eight feet by eight feet, to which Joanna headed.

"My work in progress," she said without irony. The white canvas was covered from top to bottom with black type. Joe D. dutifully began to read: *This is dummy type,* it read. *For design purposes only. It is intended to show the position of type for size and layout. This is dummy type, for design purposes only . . .* Joe D. read it twice before realizing that the message repeated itself over and over again, perhaps a hundred times. He wasn't quite sure how to respond, but Joanna Freeling's expression, confident but expectant, indicated that a response was called for.

"Interesting," he managed. Whenever he and Alison visited galleries, he noticed that she always responded to the most outlandish works—the blank canvases, the collages of shattered pottery, the S&M compositions—with a judiciously intoned "interesting."

"I'm glad you like it," Joanna said, again assuming the compliment. Like the first time he'd seen her, at Samson's funeral, she was dressed in black. This time, instead of a dress, she wore a sleeveless black T-shirt tucked into black jeans. Both served to emphasize her small but appealing figure, and her pale but not unhealthy complexion. Joe D. guessed that she was in her late twenties, perhaps early thirties. She had a thin, delicate nose, a small, roundish mouth with pale lips, and big, very dark eyes. Her thick black hair was cut short, giving her an almost pixie-like quality. She looked vulnerable and impervious at the same time, as if she possessed some superhuman power only she knew about. She was undeniably attractive, but not in an obvious way. Her appeal became apparent only gradually, but once recognized, it was erotically insistent.

"I'm applying the finishing touches, as they say. I have an opening in three weeks at the Artists Space."

She picked up a tiny brush, dipped it into a small jar of what looked like black ink, and began dabbing at the canvas, filling in the lettering where gaps were evident.

"I use a stencil to create the lettering," she explained. "Please, have a seat." She waved her brush at a black metal folding chair nearby. Joe D. remained standing. "But there are always gaps. This is my least favorite part, as you can imagine. But part of what I want to say has to do with exactness. Do you know what I mean?"

"Interesting," Joe D. offered a second time. Joanna Freeling clearly enjoyed having someone watch her at work. He was aware that he was witnessing a performance, and decided to get down to business. "Were you and your uncle close?"

She answered without breaking off from her work. "Not really. He never understood what I was trying to do."

Joanna made this sound like a devastating failure on his part.

"And yet he left you a nice chunk of money in his will."

"So I understand."

She sounded surprisingly nonchalant about so much money. "Thirty-two million is a lot of money, considering you weren't close."

"It is a lot of money, but not to Uncle George. Anyway, it's thirty-four million. The market was up yesterday."

Joe D. had to smile. "But the money must mean a lot to you."

She continued to focus on her painting. "Money isn't what I'm about."

A statement, Joe D. thought, that only a very wealthy person could afford to make. "Do you support yourself by painting?"

"Yes." Then she added, almost blithely, "plus I have an income."

"From George Samson?"

She dabbed at a capital *D.* "That's right."

Joe D. walked over to a stack of paintings leaning against the wall and flipped through them. They were similar to the one Joanna was working on, black type covering white canvases. One contained the repeated message, *If the subway stops between stations, do not get off the train. Wait for the conductor to give instructions.* Another canvas repeated this message, but in Spanish. *This has been a test of the emergency broadcasting system,* began another.

"It's all about messages," Joanna offered cryptically, joining him at the stack of paintings. "About the messages we receive from society."

He considered using *interesting* a third time, but thought better of it and changed the subject.

"When did you last see your uncle?"

"I don't know. A few weeks ago? Longer?"

She was standing uncomfortably close, Joe D. realized, and took a step back.

"Did you have plans to see him?"

She shook her head and took a step towards him. "No."

He thought about the *G* on the cabdriver's fare sheet. "The night he was killed, you had no plans to see him?"

She frowned. "Look, I don't know what Mona told you . . ."

"She didn't tell me anything, other than that you were mentioned in the will."

Joanna thought about this for a bit, then, mercifully, returned to her canvas. "The police seem to think it was a hijacking, but if it wasn't, then I'd say you should take a good hard look at Mona Samson."

Ah, Joe D. thought with satisfaction, the mudslinging has begun.

"She'd do anything for money, you know. She was born dirt-poor. In Mississippi somewhere."

"I didn't notice an accent."

"She lost that on the way."

"On the way where?"

"On the way to becoming Mrs. George Samson, queen of New York society. You might think her ancestors came over on the Mayflower, the way she talks. One thing you can say about Uncle George, he never made any bones about *his* roots. I think he was proud of them in a way. It was Mona who pushed him onto the charity circuit."

"Sounds like you don't like her very much."

Her brush froze for a moment, then resumed its dabbing at the black lettering. "Let's just say we share a mutual dislike. She disapproves of me, and I of her. She cannot stand it that George's only relative is an artist." Joe D. saw her grin slightly at this, as if she relished calling herself an artist and equally relished the effect it had on her aunt.

Joe D. reminded Joanna of her relatives in Brooklyn.

"Oh, them," she said with a shrug. "George had nothing

to do with them. Though I think he might have been amused at the fuss they made about his funeral."

"What kind of fuss?"

"It seems one of them—a second cousin, I think—found out that George was going to be cremated. That's a no-no to Orthodox Jews, apparently. They protested to Mona, who's not even Jewish, for god's sake. I think she was afraid of negative publicity—you know, 'Society queen shuns husband's poor relations'—so she gave in."

"Mona wanted him cremated. . . ."

"That's right. She'd have probably skipped the funeral altogether if it wouldn't have looked bad. Anyway, I'm the only family George was in touch with. Mona's probably got loads of family—'kin,' I believe they're called—back in Dixie, but she won't have anything to do with them."

"After Mona dies, who inherits her money?" The brush froze momentarily a second time. "I do," she said evenly, then resumed painting—or dabbing. "The shares are held in trust for me. She gets the income while she's alive, but she can't invade the principal."

She has a pretty firm grip on financial reality for an artist, Joe D. thought. "How much was your uncle paying you, before he died?"

"He didn't 'pay' me anything."

"But you said you had an income."

"That's different. Uncle George established a trust for me. I receive the dividends, which amount to about two hundred and fifty thousand dollars a year, give or take."

Trust fund or not, it still sounded like she was on her uncle's payroll. "So the thirty-two million—sorry, thirty-four million—will mean quite an increase."

"I have no plans for it. I won't move. I won't stop painting. Perhaps I'll give more to charity."

Joanna Freeling struck Joe D. as unbearably smug. He supposed you had to have a lot of confidence to spend all day stenciling gibberish onto canvases and then calling yourself an artist. Or perhaps this really was art. But weren't artists supposed to be chronically insecure? Maybe if she veered away from her "messages" into a new type of art she'd lose some of her smugness, and maybe that's why she never created anything different.

"What were you doing Wednesday night?"

"Ah, the cloak-and-dagger stuff!"

Joe D. waited for a reply.

"Actually I was at home."

"Alone?"

"No, I was with someone." Joe D. was about to ask for more specifics when she added, with, he thought, some relish, "My lover."

"Does he live here with you?"

"He has his own place. But he stays here now and then."

"Mind if I ask his name?"

"Howard Lessing."

Joe D. pulled a small pad from his pocket and wrote down the name. He asked for Lessing's telephone number. Joanna gave it to him with some impatience in her voice. "He's a writer," she volunteered. "Very talented." He thought he detected an ironically lascivious tone here.

"Did you know that your uncle had affairs?"

"You saw my aunt. Wouldn't you fool around?" she said by way of answering.

"Did you know any of his girlfriends?"

"You assume there was more than one?"

"You know otherwise?"

"No, but I wouldn't necessarily assume there was a whole string of them. In any case, no, I didn't know his girlfriends, plural or singular."

No one did, Joe D. thought morosely. He'd checked with Samson's secretary, Felicia Ravensworth, earlier that day. She was being retained by Samson Stores to help smooth the transition to the new CEO. After that, she was on her own. Felicia had seemed appalled at the idea that her late employer would cheat on his wife. "He didn't fool around," she said earnestly. "And believe me, I was in a position to know." Felicia was a short, heavyset woman who appeared to be one of the few women on Samson Stores' executive floor to take advantage of the employee discount; her dress had a polyester sheen, a cloying faddishness that Joe D., inured to the pricier goods of Alison's store, spotted instantly. Photos of her husband and children littered the top of her desk. Joe D. doubted very strongly that Samson had been having an affair with his secretary, although if he'd been searching for the polar opposite of his gauntly sophisticated wife, he'd have found it in Felicia.

Samson had been remarkably successful at keeping the identity of his girlfriend a secret, unless of course someone knew more than they were saying. "Think hard," he told Joanna. "Your uncle showed no particular affection for anyone in particular?"

"He wasn't the type," she said drily.

She stepped back a few feet from the canvas and cast an appraising glance at it. "Finished," she said with satisfaction. She looked at Joe D. "This can be really exhausting, you know. Physically and mentally."

Joe D. imagined file clerks and telephone operators felt the same way about their work.

She walked him back to the door, affording him a second look at the cavernous loft. Roller skates would be handy here, he thought. Or a golf cart. Interestingly, the vastness of the space didn't overwhelm Joanna. If anything, it flattered her, heightening, in contrast, her self-possession. How unlike the diminishing effect of Samson's huge library on Mona.

"Here's a card. If you think of anything else I should know, please call."

She walked to within three inches of him and took the card. "I may stand to gain financially from my uncle's death," she said, looking directly into his eyes. She made *financially* sound like a word you'd use to describe an advanced stage of cancer. "But money is not what I'm about."

Joe D. couldn't help glancing around the gigantic loft. In a city where space is the most precious of commodities, Joanna Freeling was sitting on a gold mine. "I'll keep that in mind," he said, and left.

Joe D. found a pay phone on the corner of Grand Street, and managed to extract from the operator the address of the Artists Space. It was just a few blocks away, on West Broadway.

The gallery occupied the entire ground floor of an old industrial building. A huge plate glass window offered a view of the immense, whitewashed space within. Joe D. opened the front door and immediately noticed a sign on the wall just to the left of the entrance.

THE ARTISTS SPACE
A NOT-FOR-PROFIT GALLERY
FUNDS PROVIDED BY:
THE NATIONAL ENDOWMENT FOR THE
HUMANITIES
AND
THE NEW YORK ART ALLIANCE

Joe D. couldn't help smiling. It looked like Joanna Freeling's upcoming gallery debut was being financed by her late uncle's pet charity. He'd debated whether or not to bother talking to someone at the Artists Space. Now he knew he had to.

He walked over to what looked like a receptionist's desk. Actually it was a white Formica countertop with a huge and luxurious arrangement of flowers on one end. He wondered, briefly, who paid for the flowers, the National Endowment or the Art Alliance. Behind the counter, perched on a barstool, was a woman. It took Joe D. a few seconds to reach the reception area, and she'd surely heard him open the door, but she didn't look up from a magazine she was reading until Joe D. said "Excuse me." She read a few more lines and then glanced up at him.

I'd like to buy every painting in the gallery, he was tempted to sneer. "I'd like to speak to the director of the gallery." Her hair was jet black and cropped to look like a silent film star's. Standing, her black dress probably came no lower than six inches above her knees; sitting, it just barely made it over her hips. He handed her a card.

He noticed a trace of interest in her expression as she read his card, but she quickly suppressed it in the interest of cool. She slithered off the stool and ambled to the back of the gallery, where she opened a door and closed it behind her. Alone in the huge gallery, Joe D. started to stroll. The exhibit was called "Open Doors"—the name was stencilled on the wall above the receptionist's desk, along with the name of the artist: Paco. No last name (or perhaps no first), just Paco. Paco had constructed a series of life-size doors, perhaps twenty in all. They were lined up along the gallery's walls, looking almost functional. Joe D. tried to open one of the doors, figuring it was probably fake. But it opened to reveal a surprisingly realistic painting of a suburban backyard, recessed a few feet behind the door. There was a small patio with a table and chairs, a bicycle lying on its side, a small, neat garden, and, visible on the near horizon, several other houses with yards doubtless identical to this one. Paco was obviously a very accomplished painter. The landscape was extraordinarily well-executed and the perspective had been perfectly rendered to achieve an uncanny realism: Joe D. almost felt as if he could step through the door. He closed it and felt momentarily disoriented. Then he tried another. The contrast couldn't have been more dramatic. This one was a recessed rendering of a long apartment-house corridor, lined with door after door. Again, Joe D. had the sensation of being able to step through the actual door into the artificial space. He closed this second door with a sense of relief, though he couldn't help being impressed with Paco's skill. The receptionist had returned to the exhibit area and was walking towards him, still in no apparent hurry. "Ms. Dixon will be right with you," she said, then detoured around him and returned to her post.

A moment later he heard footsteps. Ms. Dixon had emerged from the gallery's only functional door (other than the entrance). She was a tall, very thin woman, in her thirties, Joe D. guessed. Her hair was curly and, in contrast to the receptionist's, mercifully unruly. Her wide smile, as she approached Joe D., was another welcome change.

"Mr. DiGregorio? I'm Rose Dixon, director of the Artists Space." She extended a hand.

Joe D. thanked her for seeing him.

"Now, what can I possibly do for you?"

"I'm looking into the George Samson murder." He saw her eyes widen. "And I've just been talking to Joanna Freeling, Mr. Samson's niece."

She took a deep breath. "We'd better talk in my office, if you don't mind."

She led him back through the gallery to the door from which she'd emerged—Joe D. was almost surprised when she walked through it. It opened onto a short hallway, off of which was her small, windowless office. Posters of past exhibits lined the walls. Every horizontal surface was piled with books, catalogs, and papers. Her cluttered office made a sharp but pleasant contrast to the rather stark gallery. Rose sat behind her desk—a slab of Formica supported by two metal trestles—and he took the only other chair, across from her.

"I thought George Samson's death was random," she said.

"It probably was. I've been hired by his successor at Samson Stores to make sure."

"You don't really suspect Joanna of having anything to do with it, do you?"

Joe D. assured her he didn't. "But I do need to know as much as possible about her relationship with her uncle."

"I still don't know what that has to do with the Artists Space."

Joe D. liked Rose Dixon, but he thought she was playing dumb. She had an approachable, user-friendly face and big, bright brown eyes that seemed incapable of subterfuge. "Joanna told me she has an exhibit coming up here."

"That's right. This summer."

"Summer must be your slow season."

She smiled, understanding where he was headed. "Actually, we get a lot of tourists during the summer months."

"But not serious collectors. I noticed your gallery is funded by the New York Art Alliance."

"That's correct."

"And their biggest donor is . . ."

"George Samson," she interjected. "Look, I know what you're after. You're trying to imply that Mr. Samson strong-armed us into exhibiting his niece."

"I was only trying to find out . . ."

"Of course he did," she interrupted a second time. "That's the way the art world works. It's no different from Wall Street or Hollywood or any other field."

"It's not *what* you know. . . ."

"Exactly."

"Then what's your assessment of Joanna's talent?"

Rose hesitated. "Between us?"

Joe D. nodded.

"She's awful. *Awful.* I'm taking my entire three weeks' vacation during July so I won't have to look at those dreadful . . . *things* every day."

"Did you have any choice in whether to exhibit her?"

"Oh, there's always 'choice.' No one from the Alliance told me I *had* to show her work. It's all very discreet. You know, would I mind taking a look at the portfolio of a very talented young artist who just happens to be related to our biggest benefactor. It must be like when the Mafia asks you for a donation to the Daughters of St. Cecilia or something."

"What do you know about Joanna?"

"Her background, you mean?"

Joe D. nodded.

"Actually, we've spent quite a bit of time together. I usually do that with the artists we feature here. I need to publish a short bio for our catalogs. But it also helps us hang a show properly if we have a feel for the artist's personality. At first I dreaded spending time with Joanna. I didn't like her paintings and I usually find that if I don't like someone's work, I don't like their personality. Not to mention the fact that I didn't like having her forced down our throats. But there is something compelling about Joanna."

Joe D. thought he knew what she meant. "It's her confidence. It may be a mask, but it's hard to resist."

"Exactly. It pulls you in, and pretty soon you're seeing things through her eyes. She's had a surprisingly rough life, you know. Her father died when she was a little girl, in a car accident, I think. Her mother died of cancer just six or seven years ago. They never had much money. Her uncle only acknowledged her after both her parents were dead. Before that he wanted nothing to do with her. Some sort of family feud, I think."

"He didn't talk to any of his family."

"From what I gather, Joanna basically threw herself at her uncle's mercy. She'd just graduated from college; Carnegie-Mellon, I think. He set her up in that enormous loft of hers, and I suppose he gave her enough money so that she didn't have to work. The irony is, she might have been better off with a job. She's got a lot going for her, and if she didn't have a rich uncle she might have found out what she's good at. It certainly isn't art."

"Did she describe her relationship with her uncle?"

"I gather it wasn't too smooth, but then they'd only met seven years ago. She tended to condescend to him, I think. Talked about him as if he were some sort of baboon who just happened to make a lot of money. It's one of her least attractive qualities, this superior attitude. It's also unwise to bite that hand that feeds you."

Rose Dixon escorted Joe D. back through the gallery. "The artist who created these doors? He spends up to six months on each one. This is his first major show, and he's well into his forties. He works as a bicycle messenger part-time to support himself. I think about him whenever I'm tempted to feel too sorry for Joanna Freeling."

Joe D. agreed that she was hard to pity. "Have you sold any?"

"Two, actually. Not enough for Paco to quit his messenger job, but the show has a few weeks left to run."

They shook hands near the entrance. "We're planning a big opening bash for Joanna this summer. Underwritten by you-know-who. Maybe I'll see you then."

Joe D. laughed. "Somehow I don't see her inviting a private detective who's been nosing around her life. But if she does, I'll be there."

EIGHT

Joe D. walked uptown from the Artists Space. Soho became the Village at Houston Street, then the Village dissolved into Gramercy Park, which tapered into Murray Hill. Eventually he reached Midtown and then the Upper East Side. Home. He hadn't planned on walking the entire way, but the succession of neighborhoods exerted an irresistible pull. He was still new to the city, which had always seemed like another planet to him, though he grew up just sixty miles away. New York was everything that Waterside, Joe D.'s hometown, was not: big, sophisticated, sometimes dangerous, often impersonal, lively, frenetic, walkable. He'd always figured that Manhattan would be an easy place to get to know, with its orderly grid of streets and avenues. But the grid masked a very subtle pattern of neighborhoods and neighborhoods within neighborhoods. Within five blocks of Joe D.'s apartment were five dry cleaners, three newspaper and cigarette stands, two diners, three pharmacies, two Korean markets, two video stores, and restaurants of half a dozen cuisines. The stores you selected from among this vast local choice were the real determinant of which neighborhood you lived in. It determined the faces you saw every morning, the blocks that became so familiar you recognized every stoop, every window box. It determined the likelihood, even, that fate would send a stray bullet or a homicidal maniac in your direction. When he moved in last fall, Joe D. thought he'd never feel comfortable. He was beginning to think he was wrong.

The message light was blinking when he entered the apartment. In the past, the steady red light had been a reproach to him each time he opened the front door. Blinking, it made him feel productive, necessary.

He pressed the "play" button. "This is Seymour Franklin. Please call me as soon as you can." Franklin then gave a number that Joe D. didn't think was his office. Strange, since it was only 4:00.

Joe D. decided to change before returning the call. Alison had urged him to invest in a few suits, but Joe D. insisted on wearing his "regular" clothes on assignments. He usually wore a white or blue button-down shirt when he was working, along with a pair of black or blue jeans. He took off the white oxford he was wearing and put on instead one of the faded T-shirts he favored.

Franklin answered after three rings. "Have you made any progress?" he asked after Joe D. introduced himself.

Joe D. filled him in, wondering if Franklin would consider what he'd learned "progress."

Apparently he didn't. "That's nothing new," he said dismissively. "Mona is a cold bitch and that Joanna Freeling is a no-talent slut."

The was a bitterness in Franklin's voice that Joe D. hadn't heard before. "What's going on?"

"I'm fired, that's what. Mona Samson sent her legal goons over to my office this morning to escort me off the premises.

Apparently she didn't have to wait for the will to be probated to start exercising her control. The bitch."

Joe D.'s first thought was mercenary: Would this mean the end of his job too? "What does she have against you?"

"Against me personally? Only that I'm a grubby merchant who she had to rub shoulders with once in a while at retail industry charity events. Mona wants to wring every last cent from Samson Stores, even if it means damaging our long-term prospects. We need to be investing in store remodelings, better inventory systems, new point-of-sale technology. That takes cash. George knew this. Wall Street knows it. But not Mona. She's interested in jacking up the dividend to support her life-style."

"There must be enough money already."

"For people like Mona there's never enough. She pays more for a single dress than most Americans make in a year. She employs more household staff than the average small business. George used to complain that she bought antiques the way some people buy lottery tickets. Compulsively. Even with four houses, there aren't enough rooms for all the crap she buys. George told me she wanted a place in Paris. Maybe she needed someplace to stash her loot, I don't know. George put his foot down."

"So she had you fired to jack up the dividend to buy more dresses and antiques?" Joe D. was a bit skeptical. "As the owner, couldn't she just, I don't know, order you to raise the payout?"

"She knew I'd fight her. I never even kowtowed to George, and he was notorious for his short fuse. Mona's greed gets in the way of everything. It's not necessarily a question of needing it, mind you. It was a question of keeping score, of money for money's sake. Now that she's in control she's cashing in. And I'm out."

Joe D. took a deep breath. "Does this mean that you want me to stop?"

"On the contrary. Now more than ever we need to find

out who killed Samson. My contract has two years left on it, so I'll be able to afford you, if that's what you're wondering."

That was exactly what Joe D. was wondering.

That night Alison prepared her Frigidaire Surprise, which consisted of everything in their refrigerator not yet in an advanced stage of decomposition, sautéed in olive oil and tossed on whatever pasta they had lying around. They opened a bottle of white wine and even lit a candle.

"It's good tonight," Joe D. said after a few bites. "The bits of moo shoo pork you threw in really make a difference."

Alison smiled. "I wish I had time to do some real cooking."

"This is real," Joe D. protested.

"Real what?"

This stumped him. He left the table and retrieved a piece of paper from his office, which during meals was relocated from the dining area to the living room couch. He handed it to Alison. "Recognize any of these names?"

She glanced over the list. "This one's head of a big insurance company, I don't remember which. Other than that . . . who are these guys?"

"They're the directors of the New York Art Alliance. They were with Samson the night he was killed."

"You think one of them's involved?"

"I don't know if anyone's involved, other than some thug after a couple of bucks. But I have to assume it's more complicated than that. Otherwise I'd be out of a job. As for these guys, who knows? I have an appointment tomorrow with the head of the organization, Stuart Arnot. Maybe he'll be able to shed some light on Samson's mood that night, his relations with the other directors."

"Such a busy detective. Have some more Surprise."

Later, in bed, Alison read that morning's newspaper while Joe D. started in on Alison's paperback of *Bonfire of the Vanities.*

After a few pages he put it down. "You know, maybe it's time to think about a larger place. Now that I have some real work, this apartment's feeling kind of cramped."

"It's nice to hear you sounding optimistic," Alison said, without turning away from the paper.

"Well, we can't live here forever, not with me working on the dining room table."

Alison said nothing, which was always a bad sign.

"What's bugging you?"

"Nothing," she said, but the two syllables told him something was wrong.

"Alison, what's wrong?"

She waited a moment, then put down the paper. "You really want to know?"

She issued this as a challenge. He knew that if he answered, he'd have to lie, so he said nothing.

"How can you talk about moving when we're not . . ."

He could finish the sentence for her, and wished he'd never brought up the topic of a new apartment.

"When we're not even married," she finished after a short, emotional break.

"Why do the two things have to be connected?"

"You know they are."

He did. The subject of marriage simmered just below the surface of their relationship, invisible but threatening, like high blood pressure. He could feel it assert itself whenever they had an intimate moment or an angry argument.

"I promised myself I wouldn't bring up the subject until we were living together for a year," Alison continued. "But then you talk about getting a new place like we were roommates or something, and I can't help it."

"I shouldn't have brought it up," he offered weakly.

She got out of bed and headed for the bathroom. "I'm too old to be living with someone."

The bathroom door closed between them. Alison was thirty-seven, Joe D. just thirty-two. The age difference meant a lot to Alison, but not to him. He found Alison the most attractive woman he'd ever known. He still couldn't get used to her. Some nights he'd awaken and roll over and just stare at her in the shards of neon light leaking in through her curtains. He loved the way her face looked at these times, planes of shadow, sharply defined angles, soft, textured skin. Joe D. had first met Alison in the summer, when her face was slightly tanned, and small freckles dotted her nose. Now she'd lost her tan and he thought she looked even better, her pale complexion accentuating the luminous green-brown of her eyes, the fullness of her lips, the rich red-brown of her hair.

It was kind of ironic, her wanting to get married. When they first met it was Joe D. who pursued her. She had flinched from every emotional advance until her resistance just eroded. Now that she'd surrendered, however, her need for reassurance, for commitment, was almost overwhelming, and Joe D. found that he was the one flinching.

Alison's father had left her mother for a much younger woman when Alison was in college. She always blamed this for her skittishness about relationships, her reluctance to plunge in and, once in, her fear of being abandoned. But Joe D. suspected it went deeper. He figured there was something about being an only child, the seesaw of smothering attention and loneliness, that made her approach every serious relationship with a self-defeating skepticism.

Sometimes he thought he should just swallow hard and marry Alison: He loved her, and when he thought about his future, which was something he did often lately, it always included her. So why couldn't he do it? Damned if he knew. He had his own brand of skepticism, he supposed. His parents had never divorced, but they hardly had a close relationship. Their most typical form of contact had been a kind of half-serious bickering that Joe D. and his younger sister, now a nurse on the Island, had often joined. Then, almost fifteen years ago, his father, a Waterside cop, had been shot in the stomach during a bank robbery by an amateurish but desperate junkie. The bullet pierced his small intestine, which was reparable, and shattered his lower spine, which was not. His father had been confined to a wheelchair for the rest of his life, and the bickering turned from half-serious to completely bitter. Joe D. had read somewhere that people tend to marry a version of their most difficult parent. He recognized this as pop psychology, but still occasionally wondered which parent had been the most difficult, his father, whose moods had grown darker every year, or his mother, who sparred with his father but basically put up with his torment year after year, swallowing her frustrations, but making herself an object of pity and source of guilt in the process. Was Alison a version of either of these two people? And would marriage mean adopting one of these roles himself? Pop psychology, true—but it was almost irresistible.

Alison returned from the bathroom and switched off her reading lamp. She got back into bed, her back turned away from him. After a few moments he turned off his light and shimmied over to her. "I love you," he whispered into her ear, then nuzzled the back of her neck, which he knew she loved.

"I get so scared," she murmured. He could feel her shiver. "I have this fear that you'll leave."

"I'm not leaving, Alison."

"Not today. Not even soon. But a year from now, two years. When I think about it, about your leaving . . ."

"I'm not leaving," he repeated. But her body didn't relax until nearly fifteen minutes later, when she fell asleep. Joe D. lay awake, wishing there was some way, other than the way she wanted, to reassure her.

NINE

The New York Art Alliance was headquartered in a huge limestone building just off Central Park West. It bespoke money rather than art, and was decidedly better kept than its neighbors, even in this well-kept neighborhood.

Joe D. opened the heavy wrought iron and glass front door and entered an imposing lobby. He noted the sweeping staircase, the immense crystal chandelier, the lustrous marble floor—but failed to spot a single painting or other piece of art. Off to one side, through an open door, he saw a woman sitting behind a wooden desk. He crossed the lobby: The sound of his heels on the marble floor echoed sharply throughout the two-story entryway.

"I'm looking for Stuart Arnot," he told the woman. She was pretty and preppy and probably vastly underpaid. But something in her confident-bordering-on-smug expression told Joe D. that she was highly gratified to be working in such close proximity to the art world, if not to art itself.

She smiled and picked up the phone. "A Mr. DiGregorio to see Mr. Arnot," she said. A moment later she replaced the receiver. "Mr. Arnot's secretary will be down for you in a few minutes. Won't you have a seat." She gestured towards a sitting area adjacent to her desk.

Joe D. decided to look around instead. Her desk sat at the front of a semicircular room, off of which were several small but elegantly appointed offices. As Joe D. passed each office, its inhabitant looked up at him, rather startled, he thought, as if unaccustomed to visitors. Like the receptionist—like the building itself, for that matter—they were a well-groomed bunch, male and female, with the self-satisfied air of people who were enormously pleased to be just where they were.

"Where do they keep all the paintings?" Joe D. asked the receptionist when his tour was complete.

She looked understandably put off by the question. "We *support* the arts," she said, as if this were self-evident. "We don't actually display art. The Alliance develops programs for art education in the public schools, tours of our museums . . ." She said "our museums" as if she and her coworkers were part-owners " . . . Lecture series, multimedia presentations. That sort of thing."

"Was George Samson a major contributor?" Joe D. asked. She seemed about to answer when another women appeared in the doorway.

"Mr. DiGregorio? I'm Estelle Ferguson, Mr. Arnot's secretary. Won't you come this way?"

Estelle Ferguson was somewhat older than the receptionist, but just as tastefully turned out. She too exuded an air of satisfaction, as if she were pleased and relieved to be able to earn money while keeping brute commerce at arm's length. She wore an off-white silk blouse and a fashionably short black skirt. Alison had told him once that of all the parts of a woman's wardrobe, the shoes were the best mirror of personality. Estelle Ferguson's shoes were on the flat side and perfectly polished, more sensible than fashionable. Joe D.

followed her back into the entryway and up the wide marble staircase. She walked briskly, her left hand gliding along the thick marble handrail, which she had to know was immaculately clean. At the top of the stairs she turned left and led him down a long, narrow corridor, at the end of which was a small sitting area and a secretary's desk. She knocked softly on a polished mahogany door and opened it without waiting for a response. Joe D. entered the room. "Mr. Arnot," she said, motioning across the room. Then she shut the door behind him.

Arnot's office was the kind of room in which Joe D. had always pictured the robber barons of the last century making their unholy deals. It was panelled in some sort of rich, dark wood, with a wall of books opposite three oversized French doors that opened out onto a narrow balustrade. There was upholstered furniture at one end grouped before an immense fireplace that could accommodate a large roasting boar. A closed door off to the side probably led to a private bathroom or conference room. A massive wood desk was positioned opposite the fireplace. In between was a vast oriental rug in deep reds and blues.

Stuart Arnot struck Joe D. as surprisingly diminutive; he was almost lost in this rather grand setting. When he stood to greet Joe D., his waist failed to top the desk. He extended his arm across the desk to shake Joe D.'s hand, barely reaching it. He was bald on top, with dark brown hair on either side of his head. His pale complexion and round, rimless glasses lent him an air of studiousness. He was wearing a conservative tie, a white shirt, and suspenders. His jacket was draped over the back of his chair. The top of his expansive desk, Joe D. noticed, was perfectly neat, with two piles of papers at one end and a leather blotter in the center on which a pen and a single piece of paper were resting.

"Won't you have a seat," Arnot said. Joe D. sat in one of the two chairs that faced Arnot's desk. He expected Arnot to join him—the more important the executive, Joe D. had noticed, the more likely he was to join his guest on the visitor's side of the desk—but he remained where he was. The distance between them felt enormous.

"I guess your secretary told you why I'm here."

Arnot shook his head. "Terrible business," he said gravely.

"Was George Samson a major contributor?"

"One of our leading contributors. And a close friend, I might add." His voice was pinched and on the nasal side, as if each word was pronounced with some effort.

"The night he was killed, he attended a board meeting here, is that right?"

"Correct. We meet on the second Wednesday of each month in our boardroom, just down the hall. The meeting began at eight and ended about ten-thirty. As I told the police last week," he added testily.

"You say you meet every month at the same time. So anyone could have found out that Samson was going to be here that night."

"That's correct."

"Did you notice anything strange about Samson that night?"

"Not a bit. After all, he didn't know he was going to be hijacked."

"Did the other board members leave with Samson?"

Arnot appeared to think about this for a few moments. His right hand readjusted the pen on his blotter, so that it lay perfectly perpendicular to him. "Actually, George was the last to leave. He and I had a few words after the meeting was officially over."

"Words?"

"George Samson served as the president of our board. I merely wanted to brief him on some issues that I didn't think appropriate for the entire board."

"How much later did Samson leave?"

"Oh, maybe fifteen, twenty minutes after the others."

That jibes with what the police reported, Joe D. thought. Samson's time of death was between eleven and eleven-thirty, according to the autopsy.

"When did you leave the building that night?"

"About ten minutes after George. I brought some papers back to my office, retrieved my raincoat, then locked up."

"You didn't see Samson get into a cab?"

"No, he was long gone by then."

"How did Samson usually get home from these meetings?"

"You mean, did he usually take a taxi? No, he usually had his driver waiting."

"And you, how did you get home that night?"

"I walked to Central Park West and hailed a cab."

"And you took it to your home?"

"That's right."

"Where do you live?"

"East Nineteenth Street."

Gramercy Park, Joe D. noted. He decided this line of questioning wasn't heading anywhere. "How does Samson's death affect the Art Alliance?"

"Affect us financially?"

Joe D. nodded.

"We are well provided for in George Samson's will. He established a very generous trust."

"So you'll be receiving more now from Samson than while he was alive?"

Arnot visibly flinched at this. "Somewhat more, perhaps. But I hope you're not suggesting . . ."

"I understand Samson had a girlfriend," Joe D. interrupted. "Any idea who it might be?"

Arnot looked incredulous. "*I* certainly wouldn't know. Ours was a professional, not a personal, relationship. In any case, George didn't seem the type to have an affair."

"That seems to be the consensus."

"He was devoted to his work, his business. There was nothing frivolous about George Samson."

"Affairs aren't necessarily frivolous," Joe D. pointed out. Arnot smiled, unconvinced.

"Thanks for your time," Joe D. said. There didn't seem much point to prolonging this interview. Arnot was answering all of Joe D.'s questions, but he wasn't volunteering anything. A sanctimonious air hung over the entire Alliance building, an air that was threatened by a visit by a private investigator. "Here's my card, in case you think of anything else."

Joe D. stood. Arnot remained seated, but he did manage to press a button on his telephone. A moment later Estelle Ferguson appeared.

"Please show Mr. DiGregorio the way out," Arnot said.

Joe D. told her he could find his own way, but Estelle Ferguson insisted on accompanying him. Joe D. walked next to her this time and noticed that, while pretty, she looked extremely tense, her face almost rigid.

"You been working here long?" he asked her.

She answered without looking at him. "Three years. Mr. Arnot hired me when he joined the Alliance as director."

"What did he do before that?"

"I'm not really sure. Something in the fashion industry, I think."

"Fashion? I'd have thought they'd want an art expert."

"Oh, no. His position is really more administrative. The other employees, they're the art authorities."

"Still, it seems a big leap, from clothing to art."

"Mr. Samson recommended him for the job. I believe they met on Seventh Avenue."

She made the garment district sound like a distant and only semi-inhabitable planet. "So Samson got Arnot the job."

"He's quite capable," Estelle said a bit defensively.

"I'm sure he is. You said his work is administrative. . . ."

"Well, mostly he focuses on fund-raising."

They were at the entrance now. Joe D. opened the door.

"Mr. Arnot has done really well in the fund-raising area. Our endowment has tripled since he joined."

She seemed reluctant to let Joe D. go.

"George Samson must have been a big part of that."

"We have many other benefactors," she said. Again, Joe D. detected a slightly defensive edge to her voice.

"But none as generous as Samson, am I right?"

She shrugged. "Thank you for visiting us," she said with sudden brightness, as if Joe D. had stopped by for tea. He left the building and heard the door rattle as Estelle Ferguson closed it behind him.

TEN

Joe D. took a crosstown bus to the East Side and changed into running gear. Then he headed back towards Central Park, crisscrossing the streets and avenues to maintain his rhythm. At several corners he had to jog in place, intervals in which he felt like a complete asshole and wondered if he shouldn't reconsider the health club. The feel of that body under his foot wouldn't leave him, however. He'd jog until it did.

He reached Fifth Avenue in the Eighties, and realized he was just a few blocks from Mona Samson's building. The midday sun was surprisingly warm for late April, and he was depressingly winded for so short a run, so Joe D. decided to turn this into a business trip. He rested for a few minutes at the corner to regain his breath, then approached her building.

He recognized the doorman from his last visit. An Irishman, Joe guessed. His name tag confirmed this: M. Moran. Odd—you rarely saw any blacks as doormen in New York;

didn't matter what part of town you were in. Lots of Spanish, some Irish, few blacks.

Moran appeared to wear his uniform proudly, as if he were guarding a national landmark, perhaps Fort Knox. His hair was perfectly white, his eyes a pale blue, and his expression a mixture of suspicion and superiority.

"Are you here to see Mrs. Samson?" he greeted Joe D., showing off his doorman's memory.

"Well, not exactly. Actually, I'd like a word with you."

Two white eyebrows jerked upward.

"It's not that I want to speak ill of the dead," Joe D. began awkwardly.

"Mr. Samson was a fine gentleman," Moran said with a defensive edge.

"And popular too, with the ladies," Joe D. offered, then decided to cut the bullshit. "Look, what I'm getting at is this. I'm a private investigator. I've been looking into Samson's death. And I've discovered that he had a girlfriend."

Moran didn't react to this.

"And the reason I wanted to speak to you was to see if you had any idea who this woman is."

Moran spoke evenly. "You would hardly expect the man to bring his lady friends here, now would you?"

Joe D. had thought of this, but Samson and his wife had had several houses in addition to the apartment: One in the Hamptons, another in Palm Beach, a ski place in Colorado. Perhaps when Mona was away, George took a few risks. "Even when Mrs. Samson was away?"

"He never brought any lady friends here. Not that I'd tell you if he had." Moran flashed him an indignant look.

"And there were no packages left for pickup?"

"Packages?"

"You know, addressed to women. You seem to have an excellent memory for names."

Moran couldn't suppress a grin. "Other than the occasional business envelope, no. Not that I'd tell you if there had been."

"You're a good man, Moran," Joe D. said. He started to turn in the direction of the reservoir.

"When I like a person, and that person treats me fairly, you won't find me speaking ill of them, dead or alive."

Joe D. prepared himself for a discourse on the ethics of door watching.

"But when a person treats me badly, I find my professional ethics sorely tested."

Joe D. turned. Moran gave him a half smile, unwilling to take the next step on his own. Joe D. took it for him. "And someone in this building treats you badly, right?"

Moran nodded almost imperceptibly.

Joe D. easily guessed who. "Is that person Mona Samson?"

Moran puckered his lips as if savoring what he was about to say. He took a step toward Joe D. and almost whispered. "Like dirt. Like worse than dirt. Never a thank-you; no matter that I stood out in the pouring rain for fifteen minutes trying to hail her a cab. She was that way with all the staff, still is. And cheap? Ten dollars I get at Christmas—even Mrs. McCrory on the eleventh floor gives more than that, and her husband's in jail for securities fraud. Many's the time I thought to tell Mr. Samson about . . ."

Moran stopped short and took a deep breath. More encouragement was needed.

"What would you have told him?"

A short hesitation, then: "About her gentleman friend."

"Are you telling me she was having an affair?"

"What they did upstairs is none of my concern," he said, glancing heavenward. "All I know is he visits almost every day in the afternoons. Wednesdays, when I do the evening shift, sometimes he comes then too, but only if Mr. Samson was out of town. Dougherty, who covers the graveyard shift after me, he says this fella spends the entire night. You draw your own conclusions."

"What's this guy's name."

"Williams."

"First name?"

"Never says. Just, 'Mr. Williams to see Mrs. Samson.' "

Joe D. figured there had to be several pages of Williamses in the Manhattan phone book. And Mona Samson's Mr. Williams might not even live in New York. For that matter, Williams might not be his real name.

"What does this guy look like?"

"Tall, thin. Handsome, I guess. Younger." He spat the last word with relish.

"Younger than Mona Samson."

"By a good ten years or more." Moran couldn't help smiling at this.

"He wouldn't be up there now?"

Moran shook his head. "Neither is she."

Joe D. thought for a moment, then took out a card. "I know this is asking a lot, but how would you like to call me next time this Williams fellow shows up?"

Moran appeared to mull this over. "I don't know," he said tentatively.

"I don't have any money on me, but if you did call I'd be happy to compensate you for your trouble."

"I don't want your money," Moran said angrily. "If you think the cops got it wrong, that Mr. Samson was killed by someone he knew, then I'm only too happy to help out. If Mrs. Samson and her boyfriend are involved, so much the better. Seeing her carted off in handcuffs will be reward enough."

"If I'm not in, you'll get my answering machine. I'll call in for messages if I'm out."

Moran hesitated, then took the card and slipped it into his jacket pocket. Then he turned away from Joe D., resuming his pose of dignified superiority. "Good day, then, Mr. DiGregorio," he said flatly, as if the conversation hadn't taken place.

* * *

Joe D. walked a block north, headed into the park, and started jogging when he hit the reservoir. He spent the first lap, a mile and a third, thinking about the possibility—the reality—that Mona Samson had a lover. It was hard to imagine her drumming up enthusiasm for something as strenuous as an affair. She was fleshless and brittle, and probably not much softer inside. It was harder still to conceive of someone who would want to have an affair with her. Still, there's a lid for every pot, as his mother was fond of saying. And maybe it was money this Williams was after. For some people, money's the strongest aphrodisiac.

If Mona had a lover, that gave her a second motive for killing Samson. Love and money, purest motives there are. Then again, if she had a lover, he had a motive too. Add another suspect to the list. Last name: Williams. First name: just Mr. at this point.

Central Park sparkled that afternoon. The magnolias and cherries were just past their bloom, their petals littering the jogging trail like ticker tape after a parade. The water in the reservoir looked cool and inviting through the chain link fence, and the skyscrapers and apartment houses that lined the park appeared neat and orderly, and seemed to hint at a world beyond that was equally tidy. This was all an illusion, but a satisfying one. Joe D. decided to do a second lap.

He thought about last night's argument with Alison and wondered how they'd resolve it this time. They had barely spoken that morning as they went about their separate routines. Alison was cordial enough but distant; this was acceptable in the morning, when both were too distracted to deal with it. But later they would have to confront the issue, and Joe D. just didn't see any way out around it.

He finished the second lap, for a total of almost three miles, plus the distance between his apartment and Mona Samson's. Alison used to be an avid jogger until she opened Many Fetes. Now she only had time to jog on Sundays, and was often too tired to bother, while he was turning into the jogging enthusiast. Once he had pursued her, now he was the one holding back. Things had certainly changed in the past six months.

ELEVEN

When he got back to the apartment, the message light was blinking. In the old detective movies that Joe D. enjoyed the private eye always had a sassy, underpaid secretary sitting outside his office. He had an electronic box—cheaper, with fewer hassles, but not much in the way of companionship. Joe D. hoped the message was from Moran. It wasn't. "Mr. DiGregorio? This is Estelle Ferguson, from the New York Art Alliance?"

Her voice, nervous, almost breathless, was just barely audible above background noise. Joe D. guessed she was at a pay phone.

"I've thought about your visit this morning." A long pause full of roaring buses, car alarms, jackhammers, and honking horns. Joe D. was grateful for answering machines that accommodated unlimited messages. "There are a few things I think you should know. I didn't want to say anything to you earlier, but now . . ." Another noisy hesitation. "You can call me at the

Alliance, but if I don't answer, please say you're from . . . say you're from the groomers. My dog's having a shampoo today." She managed a short giggle, gave her phone number, waited a few moments, and hung up.

Joe D. rewound the tape and called her back. "It's the groomer."

"I know who you are," she said gravely.

"What was it you wanted to tell me?"

Estelle Ferguson whispered. Joe D. could picture her, hunched over her desk, cupping the phone. "Not here. Not now. Could we meet later, for a drink?"

"Fine. How about one of the places across from Lincoln Center?" The Art Alliance building was just around the corner from Lincoln Center.

"Too close," she breathed, then named a bar across town, on the East Side. They agreed to meet at 6:30.

Joe D. showered and changed into his work clothes: black jeans, white oxford shirt, sneakers. He called Alison at the store and told her he'd be home late. Then he headed downtown to see Howard Lessing.

Lessing lived on Gansevoort, a pretty, brownstone-lined street in the Village. Only Lessing's building looked out of place, a six-story, white-brick eyesore that had managed to squeak through before landmark regulations put a stop to most development in the neighborhood. Joe D. pushed the button next to Lessing's name on the panel just inside the front door. There was no intercom, but Joe D. had called before leaving, and arranged to meet Lessing at 3:30. After a few seconds the inside door unlocked with a harsh, throat-clearing buzz.

Joe D. climbed two flights and knocked on Lessing's door. The corridor was poorly lit, but what Joe D. could see looked grimy. Ironically, the place smelled sharply of commercial cleanser. The door was opened by a strikingly handsome man in his late twenties or early thirties. Lessing had longish sandy blond hair, eyes that seemed to be perpetually squinting, as if never quite grasping what was going on, and a slightly too-large nose that if anything enhanced his strong, confident appearance. He was tall and lean and wore a faded green T-shirt and blue jeans.

Lessing gestured for Joe D. to enter. The apartment, he could tell at a glance, consisted of one small room and a tiny, windowless bathroom. It was dominated by a large, obviously homemade loft construction; the top was a bed, with sheets draped over the edge. Underneath was a desk, bookshelves, and storage drawers. Across the room was a small, low-slung sofa, none too clean looking. A small Formica table stood in front of a tiny kitchenette in a niche that appeared to have been gouged out of the wall. Every horizontal surface was piled with books, papers, clothing. Joe D. guessed Lessing and Joanna Freeling spent most of their time together at her place; a hundred of Lessing's studios could fit comfortably into her loft. Maybe a thousand.

"Not much, but I call it home," Lessing said apologetically. Joe D. sat on the couch. Lessing pulled up a chair from the "dining area" and straddled it, draping his arms over the back.

"I suppose you want to check out Joanna's 'alibi,' " Lessing said. He made quotes in the air with his fingers.

"You were with her the night Samson was killed?"

"That's right."

"All evening?"

"We had dinner at her place, around seven, seven-thirty. We watched the boob tube until maybe midnight. Then we went to bed."

"You stayed over?"

"As is my custom most nights."

"Bit of an improvement over this place."

"A major improvement. But then, Joanna is a major improvement over solitude."

"Did anyone stop by that night? Anyone call?"

"Not that I recall."

"You two been together long?"

"About seven months."

"How did you meet her?"

"At an art opening, actually."

"You're not an artist, though, are you?"

"In this space? I'd have to do miniatures. Actually I'm a writer."

Joe D. nodded.

"I'm working on a novel. My first." Lessing gestured to his cluttered desk, as if offering proof. "Slow going."

Lessing looked surprisingly elegant, draped over the chair. He was one of those men who could throw a jacket over a T-shirt and be allowed into virtually any restaurant in town. In the same clothes, Joe D. knew he'd be rejected as shabby. Lessing didn't look so much out of place in his tiny apartment as impervious to it, as if every molecule in his body were continuously rejecting the environment he was forced, temporarily, to inhabit.

"How would you describe Joanna's relationship with her uncle?"

Lessing appeared to mull this over. "Financial," he said at length.

"No affection?"

"None. From either side. The only heat in that family was between Joanna and her aunt."

"So I've heard."

"One thing I still don't understand, how come you're looking into this? The police are satisfied it's a random thing."

Joe D. could have told him about his meeting with Samson a few days before he died. He could have told him about Seymour Franklin's desperation to get his job back. He could have told him about his own need for three hundred dollars a day. Instead he said, "Maybe that's how it will turn out in the end. A hijacking. I'm just making sure."

"For Seymour Franklin."

Joanna must have warned him. "That's right."

"You know, of course, that he has his own reasons for hoping that Samson was killed by someone in the family."

"I'm surprised you know so much about him."

Lessing looked momentarily fazed but recovered quickly. "I'm in love with Joanna. I make a point of knowing about everything that affects her."

"How does Seymour Franklin affect Joanna's life?"

"He ran the company that paid the dividends that supported her life-style."

"And I don't know why he swallowed the fly, perhaps he'll die," Joe D. continued. Lessing smiled without amusement. "How do you support your life-style?" Joe D. asked.

Lessing looked as if he were considering whether or not to answer. "It's not much of a life-style, as I think you can see."

"Still . . ."

"I sell the odd magazine piece, write the odd press release."

And accept the odd donation from Joanna Freeling, Joe D. finished silently. He wondered if Lessing had ever earned his own keep. He doubted it: There was a soft, spoiled quality to him, a blurring around the edges, that just didn't seem suited to grubby commerce. Joanna Freeling had a similar quality, but she'd had a rich uncle. Lessing had to rely on his wits—and his good looks.

"It's not a piece of cake, going out with someone as rich as Joanna," Lessing blurted after a moment's silence.

"No?"

"Everyone assumes I'm only interested in her money."

"But she's beautiful."

"True, but when I mention that I'm seeing Joanna Freeling, people never say, 'The gorgeous brunette who paints?' They say, 'George Samson's niece?' Then they look at me like I just won the lottery or something."

"Until very recently Joanna wasn't all that wealthy." Amazing, Joe D. thought, how quickly he was adapting to the world of the Samsons. A week ago he'd have called $250,000 a year—Joanna's income from her trust fund—a fortune. Now it didn't even make her "all that wealthy."

"It's all relative," Lessing said, almost sadly. Then he perked up. "Forgive the pun," he said, and smiled.

Joe D. thanked Lessing and let himself out of the claustrophobic apartment. Out on the street, he breathed deeply, checked his watch, and decided to walk uptown to meet Estelle Ferguson. After twenty blocks his leg muscles reminded him that he'd already jogged over four miles that day, so he caught a Sixth Avenue bus and transferred to a crosstown bus at Fifty-seventh Street.

TWELVE

The bar selected by Estelle Ferguson had also been chosen, that night, by a swarm of after-work revelers. Joe D. had to fight his way to the bar through a dense crowd of men and women in expensive-looking suits with expensive-looking haircuts. He was a few minutes early. He ordered a draft beer and fought his way back to the front door, the better to spot Estelle when she arrived.

He felt out of place without a suit and tie. This was Alison's crowd, he thought, not mine. The talk all around him was of media schedules and debt-to-equity ratios and the sex lives of coworkers. Only this last topic made sense to him. Back on the Waterside police force he too had had coworkers, and they did indeed have sex lives. Now he had no colleagues, though he supposed he was a "professional" of sorts, which is what Alison seemed to want. When he was alone with her, it was easier to feel that they had a future together. It was in places like this that he became aware of the two separate worlds they inhabited. Alison felt that she could merge those two worlds, or at least bring him into her world. He wasn't so sure. It used to be they talked a lot about their different religions: She was Jewish, he was Catholic. Now religion seemed like a subtopic of some larger issue that he didn't think they'd ever really resolve. At least that's how he inevitably felt in places like this bar, crowded with young professionals unwinding after a day spent making, borrowing, lending, counting, or disbursing money.

"Hello, Mr. DiGregorio."

He turned in the direction of the voice. For a moment he didn't recognize Estelle Ferguson and felt strange being recognized here, in this alien world. "I was afraid I wouldn't find you," Joe D. said when he'd regained his bearings. "And it's Joe D."

"I don't suppose we'll be able to find a table. Maybe there's a corner in the back where we could talk."

"Can I buy you a drink?"

"I'll have a Lilet," she said after thinking it over. Joe D. had never heard of this, but relayed it to the bartender, who apparently had. He ordered a second beer and rejoined her at the far end of the bar.

"Cheers," she said, and took a dainty sip of the green-colored drink.

"You seem nervous," he said. Estelle Ferguson, though every bit as well-groomed as the other people in the bar, nevertheless looked completely out of place. She exuded a fragility that seemed threatened here. Her small but pretty blue eyes constantly darted about. She reminded Joe D. of a small bird surrounded by prowling cats. The New York Art Alliance—quiet, dignified, untainted by the smell of money, though obviously quite flush—suited her much better, Joe D. could tell.

"What did you want to tell me?" he asked, once they'd found a less noisy corner in the back of the bar.

She took a second sip from her drink. It didn't look

capable of providing much fortification. "I've been wanting to tell someone for the longest time. I just never knew whom to talk to. Then you came by and I thought maybe you would know what to do."

She stopped and looked at him, wanting encouragement. "Go on," he said gently.

She started to take a third sip, but wisely opted for a deep breath instead. "Mr. Arnot handles the finances for the Alliance, and as his assistant, I naturally get involved too. It's not very complicated. We receive funds from our benefactors, and we pass along those funds to arts groups in the form of grants. Of course, we also have expenses, including salaries. Well, many of the organizations we support are kind of obscure." She smiled uneasily. "You know, art programs for convicts with life sentences, museum tours for the blind, that kind of thing. Last year we gave two million dollars to a group of Latvian folk dancers who wanted to tour mental institutions. Still, I usually get to know the various organizations through their correspondence with us. But there's one group I have my doubts about. It's called the Caribbean League. I first came across it a year or so ago when we made our initial grant to them. Nothing large, I think it was about fifty thousand. But the grants continued, and they've gotten bigger and bigger." She took another deep breath. "A few months ago I totaled up what we've given to the Caribbean League. It's nearly five million dollars, and still growing." Her voice quivered over the amount.

"Is it unusual to give so much money to one organization?"

"We make bigger grants to other groups. Music for Minors alone gets more than that each year. It's a program for juvenile offenders," she added primly. "But the thing is, I've never heard of these people. And then a month ago I was helping prepare our annual report. We give it to our benefactors, and we file it with the New York Department of State, which regulates charities like ours. Well, there was no mention in the information Mr. Arnot gave me about the Caribbean League. I asked him about this—I figured it was an oversight—but he told me he had decided to lump it in with other donations. That's just the way he put it, 'lump it in with other donations.' I started to ask him why and he waved me out of his office. 'Some of our benefactors don't see why we should support Caribbean groups,' he said as I was leaving. Then he muttered something about Caribbeans being black, and racism, and that was that."

"Doesn't anyone check your financial records?"

"Sure. We have auditors. But they just finished their audit for last year and they didn't come up with any irregularities. The money just disappeared!"

"Have you tried to track down the Caribbean League?"

She nodded. "They're not in any of the New York phone books. They're not registered as a not for profit group with the New York Department of State."

"But you said checks were made out to them. Someone must be cashing those checks."

"But who? I mail them to a post office box here in Manhattan." She smiled awkwardly, as if embarassed by this.

"Don't the checks come back?"

"Yes, in our monthly statement from the bank. It's just like a personal account, really. Mr. Arnot handles that part."

"You've never seen a statement?"

She shook her head. "They come in a very thick manila envelope addressed to Mr. Arnot. They're always stamped 'strictly confidential,' so I don't open them. I just put them on his desk."

"What happens to the statements once he's done with them?"

"He keeps them in a locked cabinet in his office."

Joe D. figured it was unlikely that Arnot would keep canceled checks that had been used to funnel money out of the Alliance. "I guess he'd destroy the checks made out to the Caribbean League," he said, thinking out loud.

"I don't know. If we were ever audited by the state, the auditors would easily detect the missing checks by their serial numbers. It would probably be more suspicious if the checks were missing." She paused and thought about this. "No, my guess is, the checks are still in his office."

"In a locked cabinet."

"That's right."

"What's George Samson's connection to this?"

Estelle looked surprised. "I don't think there is a connection. Except that he was our board president and largest benefactor."

"You don't think he knew about the Caribbean League?"

"He may have. Our trustees are kept informed about all major grants. I doubt he knew that the funds to the League weren't being reported."

They both concentrated on their drinks for a while. Joe D. was wondering if there was a connection between Samson's death and the Caribbean League. Could Samson have perhaps uncovered the fraud, threatened to expose Arnot, and been murdered to keep him quiet? Or perhaps Samson himself had been squirreling away the five million, in preparation for his faked death.

"What was the relationship between Samson and Arnot?"

"Close, I'd say. They talked frequently on the telephone."

"How frequently?"

"Once or twice a day. Mr. Arnot also had a private line installed a few weeks ago, so it's kind of difficult, monitoring his calls."

"He installed a private line a few weeks ago?"

She nodded. "It rings only in his office."

Joe D. thought about this for a bit. "Last week, did Arnot and Samson speak more often than usual?"

She squinted, trying to remember. "Last week? They may have. It seems to me that I put through more calls from Mr. Samson than usual. On Wednesday they spoke half a dozen times, though."

Wednesday was the day Samson was murdered, Joe D. reminded himself. She must have seen his eyes light up.

"But they always talk a lot on the day of a board meeting."

"Six times?"

"Well, maybe not that often." A beat, then: "Are you implying that there's a connection between Samson's death and the the Caribbean League?"

"I doubt it."

She looked disappointed.

"Then again, there might be. Is there any way I could see those bank statements?"

"As I said, they're kept in a locked cabinet. And Mr. Arnot keeps the key with him at all times."

"You said a cabinet, not a safe, right?"

She nodded. Joe D. figured he could find his way into a cabinet without too much trouble. Getting into the New York Art Alliance building might be another story.

"How could I get into the Alliance building after hours?"

"You couldn't!" she said, horrified. A tide of red flushed up into her pale cheeks.

"Do you have a key to the front door?"

"Yes, but there's an alarm."

Joe D. remembered seeing it on his visit, a panel of numbers: To gain access without triggering the alarm, you had to push the correct sequence of numbers.

"I'll bet you know the access code."

"I do," she confessed.

"So if you were to lend me the key one evening, and give me the access code . . ."

She shook her head. "I couldn't." She drained the green fluid but continued to clutch the empty glass with both hands.

"Estelle, why did you want to talk to me?"

She looked suddenly quite sad. "I had to talk to someone."

"And now that you've talked to me, you feel better?"

"Not really."

"You feel worse, because now that you've talked this thing through, you realize that there really is something going on. So you have a choice. Either say and do nothing more, and let the fraud continue. Or let me look into it and find out for sure."

She said nothing for a few moments. Then she began to speak in a soft, distracted voice.

"My parents divorced when I was quite young," she began, as if in answer to a question. "Every other Saturday I'd meet my father at the Met and we'd stroll together through the galleries. We didn't bother with the special exhibits, we'd just wander into the permanent collection, particularly European paintings on the second floor. It was so peaceful there, so removed from the cares of the world. Those pictures became like old friends you'd see every few weeks. I felt safe and welcome there. When I was at Bennington I dreamed of working in a museum after graduation. Easier said than done. Half the girls at Bennington and a hundred other schools wanted the same thing. But I did manage to find a job at the Alliance. My father knew someone who knew someone—you know how that works. The Alliance was as close to the art world as I could get. I've thought about leaving but the truth is I've been very happy there. Safe. Until this Caribbean League thing. I feel very strongly that something evil is going on and I don't know what to do about it."

Her voice was shaking, and she gripped the end of the bar as if letting go would mean being hurled into a tornado. Joe D. guessed she was near tears. "Let me look into it," he said quietly. "You'll feel safer once you know all the facts."

"I know it must seem silly to you," she continued, despite Joe D.'s attempt to steer her back toward practicalities. "Making grants to some of the organizations we support. There was even a bit of a scandal once. Some editorial writer at the *Wall Street Journal* got hold of the fact that we'd given money to a photographer who was going to document the life of a transsexual—you know, before and after." She smiled uncomfortably, raised the empty glass to her pale lips, and took a sip of air. "Of course, the *Journal* saw this as a waste of money, and we received a lot of calls from donors, but in the end the show ran at museums all over the country and received favorable notices. I never saw the show myself, but I understand it was quite . . ."

"Help me get into the Alliance building," Joe D. cut in.

She seemed almost shocked by his interruption, and waited a few moments before nodding. She took a pen and small pad of paper from her pocketbook and wrote down a six-digit number. "Here's the access code." She fished through her pocketbook and handed him a key. It was attached to a round tag with "NYAL" written on it. "It's an extra key. I have another one. Just return it to me next week sometime. Your best bet is this weekend, at night. Weeknights, the cleaning service is there. Weekends, the place is deserted. There's only one locked cabinet in Mr. Arnot's office."

She looked like she could faint from anxiety. Her delicate skin was now drained of color, and her knuckles paled from the effort of squeezing the empty glass; Joe D. worried that she'd shatter it. "Let me buy you another drink," he offered.

"Oh, no. I couldn't. I have to go. I have an . . ." She looked momentarily overwhelmed by her inability to find an excuse. "I have to go, that's all."

She put down her glass on the nearest ledge and started for the door. A few feet away she turned, walked back to him. "If you're caught . . ."

"We never met," Joe D. obliged. She smiled weakly, turned, and hurried from the bar.

THIRTEEN

Alison didn't so much enter their apartment that evening as burst in. Just from her expression, Joe D. could tell that the cold war between them had thawed.

"You won't believe it," she said, and threw down a thick envelope of paperwork she inevitably brought home from Many Fetes.

"Try me," Joe D. offered. He figured she had finally sold the outrageously overpriced, hideously vulgar sequin-and-lace concoction he had nicknamed the "Whatever Happened to Baby Jane" dress. Alison's profit on the outfit, if she ever managed to find a buyer, could pay their mortgage for three months.

"I had lunch with Sharon Epstein today. . . ."

The name rang no bells, though he could tell from Alison's face that it should.

"I knew her from Bloomingdale's. We had dinner with Sharon and her husband, Peter, last fall. He was with Salomon

Brothers until the crash. Now they both run a personal trainer referral service."

Joe D. dimly remembered them, an attractive couple who had spent the entire evening lamenting the deterioration in the value of their cop-op off Second Avenue. "Yeah."

"Well, I mentioned to Sharon about your investigating the Samson murder . . ."

"I'm not sure that was a good idea."

"I couldn't help it. For years Sharon used to brag about Peter. Now it's my turn."

So I'm on a par with half a million-dollar-a-year investment bankers, Joe D. thought. He didn't know whether to be pleased or mortified.

"Anyway, Sharon told me this incredible story. About George Samson. It seems that ten years ago, Samson bought out a rival chain; Rudolph's, they were pretty big once, though not in Samson Stores' league. Sharon knew some of the buyers there. Anyway, no sooner did Samson buy the company than he fired the top managers and installed his own people. The founder of Rudolph's, Arthur Rudolph, went nuts. He spent the next five years trying to take over Samson Stores."

"I thought Samson owned most of the stock."

"He does. Did. That's why it was so futile for Rudolph to try and take them over. He spent millions on Samson stock, and millions more in fees to investment bankers. Apparently, he tried to convince large shareholders like pension funds to join him. But they were content with Samson's management and refused. Once his takeover bid failed, the stock started to slide. Since he'd borrowed to buy some of it, his lenders started squeezing him. He sold at a loss, and when the whole thing was over he was practically broke."

"Where's Rudolph now?"

"Sharon heard he went nuts. He's in a nursing home somewhere."

"Sounds like someone I ought to talk to."

"You think so?"

"He obviously hated Samson."

"God, this is exciting."

Joe D. had to laugh. "Maybe we should be partners."

"Rosen and DiGregorio. Has a nice ecumenical ring to it."

"DiGregorio and Rosen has an even nicer ring."

Alison turned serious. "About last night . . ."

"I'm sorry," he said.

"No, I'm sorry."

They looked at each other for a few moments, then smiled guiltily. Many of their arguments ended this way, with both apologizing. Sometimes this struck Joe D. as incredibly civilized. But tonight it seemed they were taking the coward's way out, both of them eager to assume responsibility to avoid facing the real issues.

"Let's go out to dinner and celebrate this new breakthrough," Alison suggested. "I have an urge for something spicy, maybe Thai."

"I have an urge for something spicy too," he said, and pulled her to him. They held each other for a while, reestablishing their intimacy.

"You won't leave me, Joe D.," she said over his shoulder, half questioning, half commanding.

"You know I won't."

She pulled away and looked at him, unsure but anxious to be convinced. Then she headed for the bedroom. Joe D. followed.

FOURTEEN

Joe D. called Seymour Franklin at his home Saturday morning. "What do you know about Arthur Rudolph?"

"Ah," Franklin said, stretching out the word. "So you've stumbled upon poor Arthur."

"I haven't actually talked to him. But I understand he wasn't overly fond of George Samson."

"Hated his guts, actually. Samson fired Arthur after buying out his company. Then Arthur went broke trying to buy out Samson. A sad story, really. At one time Arthur was worth forty million."

The numbers that were battered around in this case were mind-boggling, Joe D. thought. "Where is Rudolph now?"

"In la-la land, I should think. He lost his mind when he lost his money." Franklin said this matter-of-factly, as if insanity, liked bounced checks, was an unavoidable consequence of insolvency.

"He's in a nursing home, I hear."

"That's right. It's up in Westchester. Tranquility Village, it's called. Samson Stores pays the bills. George Samson said it was the least he could do. But he must have known that it would drive Arthur crazy—or crazier—to know that his enemy was paying his way."

"I think I'll drive up there today."

"Arthur's harmless. You're wasting your time."

And my money, Joe D. half expected him to add, but he didn't. Apparently three hundred dollars a day was just too insignificant to worry about. Franklin and his peers were the types who talked about *two million and change,* where the "change" was worth maybe three times Joe D.'s annual salary, back when he had a salary. "I have to follow up every lead. If Rudolph hated Samson, he's worth talking to."

"Suit yourself. Though I still think Mona Samson's your best bet."

"Did you know that Mona was having an affair?"

"Was she? Hard to imagine, don't you agree?"

"Does the name Williams ring any bells?"

"Other than Andy and Ted? None."

"Somehow I don't picture her having an affair with Andy Williams."

"No, nor Ted for that matter."

Joe D. rented a Ford Escort Saturday morning, and drove up to Tranquility Village in northern Westchester. Alison had insisted that he sell his Trans Am before moving to the city. She said that garages were just too expensive in the city, which was true enough. But Joe D. knew she felt about the car the way she'd feel about an old girlfriend who wouldn't disappear. It was a symbol of his past life, his life as a cop in Waterside, New York; a sleek, black, eight-cylinder gas-guzzler that had "blue-collar" written all over it, though it had cost Joe D. a bundle. He had hated selling the Trans Am. As he watched the buyer drive away in it, five thousand dollars in cash in his pocket, he felt his past life receding at a dizzying pace. Now, as he headed north on the Hutchinson Parkway, the Escort shimmied and shuddered whenever he pushed it past sixty, so he moved to the right land and kept to within the speed limit, and thought wistfully of his old car.

At first glance, Tranquility Village looked appropriately named. Joe D. drove through two brick columns and down a long, winding driveway lined with elms and carefully tended flower beds. The main building was a brick mansion fronted by four two-story white columns. It had probably been a private estate once. The day was warm and sunny. Old people and nurses made their way around the grounds; they walked so sluggishly, it was as if the place had been sprayed with a slow-motion drug. Joe D. slowed the car to a crawl for the last fifty yards. He pulled up to the front of the mansion, where a small visitors' lot had been carved out of the lawn. When he closed the car door, a dozen heads turned slowly in his direction.

By the time he reached the front door, Joe D. decided the place was anything but tranquil. It was sterile, stultifying, unnerving—and he hadn't even been inside yet.

The front hallway had obviously been quite elegant at one time, with a marble floor and niches on either side where statues once rested. Now the niches were empty, and a Formica desk sat squarely in the center of the space, looking resolutely inappropriate. Behind it sat a young woman in a nurse's aide uniform. She smiled at Joe D. as he approached the desk. "Good morning. How can I help you?"

This place must cost a mint, he thought, cordiality in nursing homes being more expensive than prescription medicine. "I'm here to visit Arthur Rudolph."

Some of the cordiality began to crumble. "Excuse me?"

"Arthur Rudolph. I'd like to see him."

"One moment." She picked up the phone and pressed two numbers. "There's a gentleman here to see Arthur Rudolph," she whispered into the phone. The way she said his name, it was as if Joe D. had asked to see Santa Claus. A moment later she hung up and said that the weekend manager would be out in a minute.

"I don't understand. Is there a problem?"

"Mrs. Hodgson will help you," she said crisply. It was obvious that something was very wrong.

"Is Arthur Rudolph dead?"

"You'll have to ask Mrs. Hodgson."

The all-knowing Mrs. Hodgson arrived a minute later. She was tall and thin and looked about sixty. She wore a white silk blouse with a silver pin between the collars and a long gray skirt. Her hair was also gray, pulled back tightly from her forehead into a small, hard bun. "I'm Grace Hodgson. You are . . ."

"Joe DiGregorio. I'm a private investigator looking into . . ."

"Ah, of course. Please follow me."

She led him down a short hallway into her office, which looked like it had probably been the library of the mansion. Most of the bookshelves were empty, however, except for piles of manila folders and stacks of trade magazines. The desk and file cabinets were metal, the visitors' chairs of the institutional variety. No attempt had been made to blend the present with the past. Instead, the present had been simply *applied* to the past with a willful disregard for aesthetics, the way ancient civilizations piled their new buildings on top of the rubble of earlier cities. Like the entranceway, Grace Hodgson's office had a temporary feel about it, as if it had been set up only yesterday and would be dismantled any minute to make way for the next inhabitant.

She motioned Joe D. toward a chair and sat on a matching chair a few feet away, facing him. "I was wondering when the Rudolph family would take up their own investigation," she began. "Of course, Mr. Rudolph's son was here the day after we called him, but since then we've heard nothing. We notified the local police, but they were less than helpful, I'm afraid."

Joe D. decided to back up and start with preliminaries. "Mrs. Hodgson, I'm not working for the Rudolphs."

She looked shocked. "You're not?"

He explained about George Samson's death, and briefly told her about the relationship between Samson and Rudolph.

"I know all about their relationship," she said. "Samson Stores paid all the bills."

"Did Rudolph know that?"

"I'm not sure he was aware of very much. He was only in his sixties, but his mind was quite gone."

"Where is he now?"

"That's just it, we don't know. He disappeared Wednesday morning."

"Disappeared?"

"It was a lovely day, much like today. He was sitting out on the lawn, enjoying the sun. When we called everyone back in for lunch, he was gone!"

"Was he in good enough shape to walk out on his own?"

"Possibly. But we're quite isolated here, as you can see. Even if he made it to our front gate, what would he have done then? There are no bus stops nearby."

"Could someone have picked him up?"

Mrs. Hodgson waited before answering. "Our residents are not permitted to leave the premises without signing out. And they must be accompanied by a family member or other authorized individual."

"But if someone just drove up and told him to get in the car . . ."

"Our staff-to-resident ratio is among the best in the industry," she said officiously. "Still, for those patients who are not prone to wander, and who can get about on their own, we do allow a certain degree of freedom."

"Meaning, no one was watching Rudolph Wednesday morning."

"He didn't require one-to-one monitoring."

"Do you have many visitors here during the week?"

"A few. There are also deliveries."

"So a car pulling up Wednesday morning wouldn't have attracted much attention."

"Not at all."

"Did Rudolph have many visitors while he was here?"

"His son came every few weeks. No one else."

"Has his son heard from him since his disappearance?"

She shook her head. "We haven't heard from his son since we first notified him of his father's disappearance. But he did say he'd call if his father was found. I assume he'd be returned here."

"Did Rudolph seem at all different in the days before his disappearance?"

"I asked the staff that very question. They hadn't noticed anything unusual in his behavior. He was very quiet, mind you. Kept to himself. He muttered a lot, of course."

"Did he seem angry?"

She thought about this. "I would say that he was not a man at peace with the world. His muttering had a quality of paranoia to it."

"Paranoia?"

"Oh, you know, he'd glance around him like a frightened bird, then grumble about someone out to get him, about being a victim. We never took him very seriously. He was completely deluded. But, then, things have been rather difficult for the poor man."

"Difficult?"

"Well . . ." She appeared to consider her words carefully here. "Let's just say that downward mobility may be one of life's most difficult burdens."

Joe D. could think of a few tougher afflictions: Illness and death came to mind. But Grace Hodgson seemed to have a story to tell him and he wasn't about to stifle her. "He lost all his money, apparently."

She nodded, a grave expression on her face. "You know, of course, that he's one of *the* Rudolphs."

"Which Rudolphs would those be?"

She smiled indulgently at him, as if he'd admitted to not knowing the occupant of Grant's Tomb. "Arthur Rudolph was the great-grandson of Adolph Rudolph." A pause, in which Joe D. failed to shriek with recognition. "Adolph Rudolph came to this country from Germany during the last century. He established the first Rudolph's Shop on lower Fifth Avenue. His son expanded the store, and *his* son opened several others in suburban locations. But it was Arthur—our patient," she added smugly, "who really transformed them into a major national chain. He opened Rudolph's Shops all over the country. I don't know how many there were before they were bought out. There were several right here in Westchester. They always carried such nice clothing too. Nothing too stylish, mind you, just good classic designs." Her voice had turned wistful. "Then Mr. Rudolph sold out to Samson Stores."

"Sounds like a mismatch. Samson Stores are for teenage girls."

"Girls on a budget," she added. "But that's just the point. Samson was never interested in Rudolph's for its merchandise or its reputation. George Samson only wanted the leases. Rudolph's had stores all across the country with long-term leases with years left on them. As soon as he took over, he converted all the stores to Samson's. It broke Mr. Rudolph's heart, I think. Then it broke his mind."

Joe D. had heard sadder stories, but Grace Hodgson clearly placed the demise of Arthur Rudolph on a par with *King Lear*. "How does a nurse know so much about retailing?" he asked.

"Administrator," she corrected him. "It's not that I know so much about retailing as that I make it my business to know about my patients. For starters, we run a detailed credit check on all applicants. Our fees are quite high."

"But Rudolph's bills are paid by Samson Stores."

"Exactly. So in addition to looking into Mr. Rudolph's finances, which I'm sorry to say were quite dismal, we had to check into Samson Stores as well. In particular, we had to ascertain to our satisfaction that Samson Stores would continue to pay Mr. Rudolph's bills."

"And were you satisfied?"

"Quite. And we made sure that the contractual obligation was with the corporation, not Mr. Samson personally."

"Very farsighted of you."

She smiled. "I think George Samson took a particular pleasure in destroying Arthur Rudolph. I almost hated to take his money."

This rang so untrue that Joe D. could only stare at her.

"The Rudolphs are one of the oldest Jewish families in New York," she continued. *"Our Crowd* and all that. Samson, on the other hand . . ." She paused, doubtless fishing for a way to express her scorn without sounding snobbish. "Samson was more . . ."

"More Jewish," Joe D. offered.

She made a face. "I detest it when people put words in my mouth. It's just that Arthur Rudolph was always one of New York's most prominent citizens. I remember reading about him and his wife in the society pages. Giving parties for charity, that kind of thing. They were so handsome together."

"Where is Mrs. Rudolph now?"

"She died about ten years ago. Cancer, I believe."

"About the same time Rudolph sold his company to Samson."

"Yes, I suppose that's correct. Perhaps if his wife hadn't died he would have held on."

"And perhaps if she'd been alive he wouldn't have spent every dime he had trying to take revenge on Samson."

"Yes, she might have kept him more firmly anchored."

"You mentioned Rudolph's son. Were there any other children?"

"None."

Joe D. asked for the son's name and telephone number. She consulted a bulging Rolodex and copied it down for him. "His name is Arthur Rudolph, Junior. I believe he's known as Chip. He lives in Manhattan."

Joe D. next asked to see Rudolph's room. Grace Hodgson seemed almost enthusiastic about the idea. She escorted him there in long, brisk strides. She was clearly relieved that someone was looking into Rudolph's disappearance, but her concern seemed official rather than personal. While losing a patient to death was probably no big deal at Tranquility Village, losing a live one was doubtless a serious problem. And losing such a prominent, or formerly prominent, patient was a potential public relations disaster.

Rudolph's room was in a modern annex to the main building. It was small and very neat, with a twin-sized bed in the center, a night table, a dresser, and a visitor's chair. It had a private bath.

"We've kept it for him since Wednesday, even though there's a waiting list for new residents. He's paid up through the end of the month. And of course we're hoping he comes back," she added quickly.

"Mind if I look around?"

"By all means."

Joe D. went through the dresser drawers first. Rudolph's clothes were neatly folded, doubtless by the staff. Nothing much of interest there. In the drawer of the night table, however, he found a thick stack of documents. He pulled them out. There was an annual report for Samson Stores, some financial statements for the company, and some clippings about the company, quite recent, from the *Wall Street Journal* and *Women's Wear Daily.*

"Did Rudolph subscribe to these publications?" Joe D. showed her the stack of clippings.

She shook her head. "I'm quite sure he didn't. His son must have brought them here. Or mailed them."

Joe D. thumbed through the clippings. Quarterly earnings reports, executive changes, some society notes about Samson and his wife—nothing that had to do specifically with Rudolph. Still, Rudolph was keeping up to date on his nemesis, or was being kept up to date. The clippings, even the most recent ones, had a frayed, dog-eared look to them, as if they'd been consulted over and over again. Joe D. thought about Rudolph wasting away in Tranquility Village while Samson had lived like modern-day royalty. Must have eaten him alive, he thought. And his son, Arthur Junior—Chip—couldn't have been too happy about the situation, either.

He returned the clippings to the drawer and thanked Grace Hodgson, who walked him back to the front door. "I hope you locate him, Mr. DiGregorio. We were all very . . ." A defeated look came across her face for one moment, as if she simply wasn't up to the effort of saying something that sounded sincere. "I hope you find him. Call me if you do."

Joe D. hurried to his car, anxious to escape the smothering atmosphere of Tranquility Village. The place had a falseness to it, a pretense, that he found deadening. If there hadn't been such an expensive effort to disguise what the place really was—a last resort for the aged and the infirm—he might not have minded it as much. He'd been in less posh nursing homes before and had found them depressing, but Tranquility Village was depressing in a deeper way: Its residents lived more luxuriously, but they were all the more invisible for it. He sensed that the families of the residents felt a certain self-righteous satisfaction at being able to afford this place, and that this satisfaction frequently took the place of actual visits.

Joe D. glanced in the rearview mirror at the mansion as it receded behind him, and thought that this was the kind of place George Samson might have lived in by himself, a country house. Rudolph, once his financial equal, had had to share it with dozens of senile old people and indifferent nurses.

Until he disappeared on Wednesday. The day Samson was murdered.

FIFTEEN

It was just after 2:00 when Joe D. dropped off the Escort at the rental office near First Avenue. He and Alison had plans to meet some friends of hers for dinner at 7:30. He called her at the store and left a message with her assistant that he'd join her and the other couple at the restaurant.

He walked the eight blocks to Ideal Locksmiths on Second Avenue. It was a tiny store, its walls lined with dummy keys, locks of all sizes, and any number of home-safety implements that were as much in demand in Manhattan as suntan lotion at a beach resort. Joe D. had first visited Ideal, and its owner Carmine, when he moved into New York last fall. He'd gone there to have duplicates of Alison's keys made. Carmine had asked him if he was new to the neighborhood and what he did for a living. Joe D. told him. "Not many private dicks in this neighborhood," he'd told Joe D. "You should do great here. And you ever need help with locks, installing them or de-installing them, you let me know."

In all the time he'd been in business, he'd only had to call on Carmine once. A friend of Alison's father, who owned a dressmaking company on Seventh Avenue, had hired Joe D. to investigate a rash of employee thefts. Entire bolts of expensive fabric were found missing once or twice a week. Turned out it was a salesman, and not a seamstress, as had originally been suspected, who was taking the cloth—the man had a gambling problem, and sold the bolts at half price to pay off his debts. Joe D. had nailed the guy by spending three nights hidden in the shop foreman's office. The salesman would return to the company late at night, after losing at the track, lift a bolt of fabric, and stash it in his car until the following morning, when he sold it. Joe D. presented his evidence to the owner, who winced and said that the thieving salesman was one of the company's best producers and couldn't be gotten rid of. In fact, the owner didn't even want to mention the whole affair to the salesman, lest he quit. So Joe D. had suggested locking up the fabric, and had thus involved Carmine in their first professional relationship.

"Joe D., how are ya?" the locksmith said in classic New Yorkese.

"I need some advice."

Carmine's eyes widened at the prospect. "A job?"

"It's something I gotta do on my own. There's a locked cabinet I need to get into, but I can't let the owner know I've been there."

"What kind of cabinet?"

"I don't remember exactly, but I think it's in a pretty expensive piece of furniture, something you'd see in a dining room, maybe. Except this piece is in an office."

"No problem. The more expensive the furniture, the worse the lock. You'll need a few of these." He rummaged around under the counter and produced a small box of what looked like old-fashioned skeleton keys. "There's not too much variety in these babies, so one of these should work."

There must be twenty or more keys, Joe D. thought. His heart sank at the prospect of trying each of them.

A woman walked in and took out a set of keys.

"Now, they may have installed a modern lock in the old furniture. In which case you'd need . . ." He stopped himself and turned to the customer. "Can I help you?" he said testily.

She took a key off her key ring and asked for a duplicate. He took it from her and quickly ground a new one. "Anything else?"

Only in New York, Joe D. thought, would Carmine get away with this level of customer service. The woman paid for her key and left.

"As I was saying, if it's a new lock you'll need this." He crouched and rummaged a second time under the counter and emerged with a small vinyl case. "It's a pick set. I can show you how to use it, but why don't I come along with you and do it myself."

Joe D. shook his head.

Carmine looked disappointed. "Shouldn't be much of a problem to get in. People don't install good locks in furniture. What's the point? You can always pry the sucker open if you can't get through the lock."

He gave Joe D. a quick lesson in picking a lock, interrupting his discourse, reluctantly, to help two customers. Joe D. left Carmine at close to 3:00 and took a cab over to the West Side.

Joe D. had the cab let him off on Central Park West. He walked the half block to the New York Art Alliance building. He fished the key that Estelle Ferguson had given him out of his pocket, along with the alarm code. Then he approached the building as if he had every right to enter it, ignoring the several pedestrians on the block.

He entered the building, closed the door, and immediately punched in the code on the electronic panel to the right of the entrance. A green light lit up on the LCD panel, which he took to mean that he'd either punched in the correct sequence of numbers or the cops were on the way. He waited a few moments to see if anything happened. Nothing did, so he crossed the large hallway and headed up the stairs.

Buildings always have a completely different character when they're empty. The New York Art Alliance building had first struck Joe D. as a self-satisfied kind of structure, almost smug in its well-constructed solidity. Everything about it, from the polished marble floor in the foyer to the massive bannister along the curved staircase, had seemed impervious, not merely untouched by the people who occupied it but in defiance of them. Now, empty and only dimly illuminated by fading sunlight, the building seemed oddly pathetic, its grand spaces almost ridiculous without occupants to give them purpose, life. Inhabited, the building achieved what it had been designed to do: intimidate. Empty, it revealed its true self: A big, hollow shell, needlessly grand, all dressed up with no one to impress.

The Alliance didn't strike him as the kind of place where employees worked on Saturdays—most of them probably had weekend places, he figured. But he tried to walk silently anyway, just in case there was someone working inside. The building was completely quiet. Eerily quiet: Marble and plaster and granite don't squeak like wood, so there were none of the unnerving sounds you'd expect to hear in an old building. Still, the silence was unnerving in its own way.

Joe D. headed straight for Arnot's office. The door was open, as Estelle Ferguson had said it would be. Joe D. entered the large room and looked around. Sure enough, there was a low-slung cabinet next to Arnot's massive desk. Joe D. crossed to it and smiled: The lock was of the old-fashioned, easy-to-pick variety, as Carmine had predicted. He knelt down in front of it and took out the small box of skeleton keys from the bag Carmine had put them in. Then he set about trying each of them, still careful to avoid making any noise.

By the fifth key Joe D.'s spirits were beginning to flag. What if none of the keys worked? He was considering simply prying open the cabinet, which didn't look like too big a challenge, when he turned the eighth or ninth key and felt the lock give. Is there a more delicious feeling than when a once-obstinate lock finally surrenders?

He pulled open the door. The cabinet was perhaps eighteen inches deep, divided in two by a single shelf. Bunches of paper were stacked neatly on the bottom of the cabinet and on the shelf. Joe D. picked up one stack and saw at once that the papers dealt with salary issues, personnel matters—the sort of papers any manager would keep locked up. Another stack of papers appeared to be financial statements. Joe D. flipped through them, unable to make much sense of the columns and rows of figures.

He found what he was looking for in the third pile of papers. These were the bank statements Estelle had told him about. Each statement was three pages long, folded in three, and held together by a large paper clip. Joe D. opened the statement on top, which was for the previous month. Inside were several dozen business-sized canceled checks. He flipped through them. They were made out to what were obviously arts groups, and many were quite large: Six hundred thousand to something called the Art for Seniors Program; five hundred thousand to Painting Partners in Russia. Halfway through the pile he found what he'd been looking for. One million, two hundred and fifty thousand dollars, made out to the Caribbean League. The signature was Arnot's, as it was on all the other checks. He turned the check over to look at the endorsement.

Then he felt something on the back of his head.

A tickle. No, something else. Something . . . harder. Much harder. Before he could make out what it was he was unconscious.

SIXTEEN

Joe D. opened his eyes to a swirl of colors, mostly reds and blues. He closed his eyes and his stomach started swirling. He opened his eyes. More swirling reds and blues. He repeated this process a few times until he was convinced that neither alternative was very appealing. Slowly, for he felt as if a weight had been strapped around his neck, he lifted his head. A moment later he let it fall back to the floor. He'd learned one thing at least. He was lying on the floor of Stuart Arnot's office. He had a second revelation a moment later: The swirling reds and blues belonged to Arnot's oriental rug, which was now, curiously, in orbit.

He rested a few minutes, aware that he was lapsing in and out of consciousness. Every few moments he would latch onto a new piece of information about what was happening to him, or had happened. At one point he managed to localize the source of the pounding pain somewhere to the north of his neck by running his hand gingerly along his head. He felt a lump where there hadn't ever been one, just at the base of his cranium. He carefully explored this lump with the very tips of his fingers. It appeared to be about two inches in diameter, and was as sensitive to touch as a testicle. The hair around it felt matted but dry.

Joe D. rested with this information for a while before he managed to discern another bit of news: He'd been hit from behind. Not a brilliant conclusion, but the best his puréed brain could come up with under the circumstances.

Lying on Arnot's oriental rug. Bump on the back of the head. Hit from behind. It wasn't long before Joe D. managed to weave these three facts into a coherent narrative that began with him kneeling before Arnot's locked cabinet, studying documents, and ended with what felt like the world's worst hangover.

But what specifically had he been looking at? Joe D. figured it was time to stand up and have a look around. At first his limbs didn't seem to respond. Apparently his autonomic nervous system had been extinguished by the blow to his head. Amazing that my heart keeps pumping without instructions, he thought. Happily, he found that if he gave his arms and legs deliberate orders, they obeyed—and functioned quite well at that. So he ordered his arms to push him off the floor, then told his legs to assume a kneeling position. So far so good. If only his head didn't feel like a sixty-pound dumbbell. He felt he had to concentrate on keeping it upright, lest it topple over and bring his whole body with it.

The office felt empty—certainly it was quiet. But then, it had been quiet earlier, just before someone brained him. How much earlier? Joe D. checked his watch, and at first thought that it too had been clobbered. It couldn't be 7:00. He looked more closely a second time and saw the second hand moving with infuriating regularity around the dial. It *was* 7:00. Joe D. tried to calculate how long he must have been unconscious, but this effort made his head start to pound even more viciously. He settled for a long time. He slowly looked around the office and reassured himself that it was empty. Then he focused on the cabinet.

It looked much as Joe D. remembered, discrete piles of papers stacked neatly along the bottom of the cabinet and on the single shelf. Then he recalled that he had been interested in something specific. A moment later he remembered the bank statements. He inched closer to the cabinet, still on his knees, and slowly examined each stack of papers. The bank statements were gone.

Joe D. thought about this for a while, then ordered his legs to unbend. Once standing, however, he felt himself wavering, and gratefully leaned on Arnot's desk. His lock-picking tools were spread out at his feet next to the shopping bag Carmine had given him. He stared at these objects for a while. Picking them up seemed beyond his current competence. He checked his watch again, hoping he'd misread it the first time. He hadn't. It was 7:15. Time flies when you're having hallucinations.

It's amazing what the brain is capable of even when pulverized. A moment after consulting his watch Joe D. remembered that he was supposed to meet Alison and another couple at a restaurant at 7:30. He even remembered the name of the restaurant. Caroline's. He commanded his legs to return him to the floor, where he gathered the tools into the shopping bag. There didn't seem much point to closing and locking the cabinet. If it was Arnot who had decked him, then Arnot would obviously know about the missing reports. If someone else had done it, then Arnot might as well find out right away that the statements were gone. Might be interesting to see what he did with this information.

The office was almost completely dark now, illuminated only by the faint glow of a street lamp outside the windows. Joe D. stood up and carefully crossed the room. He was aware of the possibility that his attacker might still be in the building. But he doubted it. Whoever had hit him hadn't seemed to mind that he was still alive and probably wouldn't have a change of heart now. Anyway, Joe D. knew he was in no condition to defend himself.

He located a bathroom down the hall from Arnot's office. He found a switch and flicked it on. The light sent an electric current zapping through his brain of such painful intensity it could make the most ardent death penalty advocate a foe of capital punishment. He steadied himself for a moment, and then stood before the mirror over the sink.

He'd expected to see the Elephant Man and discovered instead his old familiar mug. No sign of bruises, blood. He was almost disappointed. Then he twisted his head to either side and could just barely make out the lump. It didn't look too bad either. He dampened a paper towel and very cautiously dabbed the matted hair. He examined the towel and saw that he'd succeeded in wiping off some dried blood, which was surprisingly black. He spent another few minutes dabbing away at the lump until the towel stopped picking up much blood. He tore the towels into smaller pieces and flushed them down the toilet. He tucked in his shirt, splashed some cold water on his face, and took a second look in the mirror. He'd had better days, he concluded, and a few worse ones. Very few.

Walking down the sweeping staircase was a challenge. He took the steps one at a time, pausing every few steps to steady himself. By the time he reached the bottom Joe D. felt he could tackle anything. Well, at least he felt he could hail a cab and direct it to the restaurant. Which is what he did after locking the front door of the New York Art Alliance.

Caroline's had been favorably reviewed two weeks earlier in the *New York Times,* so Joe D. wasn't surprised to find it packed when he arrived a few minutes after 7:30. The maître d' looked at him the way New Yorkers look at homeless people, with a mixture of pity, revulsion, and outright scorn. Joe D. should have been tipped off that something was strange about his appearance, but in his experience maître d's at expensive restaurants always looked at their patrons as if they lived on the sidewalks.

He was told that his "party" was already seated and was directed to a table towards the back of the restaurant. Unfortunately, this meant navigating a small forest of tightly packed tables, a difficult task under ordinary circumstances but close to impossible now. Twice Joe D. had to grab onto chair backs to steady himself. He hoped no one noticed.

Alison's expression when she spotted him gave a more accurate reflection of the way he looked than the mirror had fifteen minutes earlier. She and her friend, Pamela something-or-other, were seated against the wall, facing out. Pamela's husband, Richard, had his back to the dining room. Pamela and Richard were both lawyers, Joe D. recalled. What he couldn't recall at the moment was how Alison knew them or if he'd ever met them before.

Alison's horrified expression intensified as he approached; he was tempted to check his fly. He managed to sit down next to Richard. Never had sitting felt so good, so necessary.

"Sorry I'm late," he said, but judging by the way the three looked at him, he might have announced that he had contracted typhoid on the way to the restaurant.

"What happened to you?" Alison whispered after a few moments.

"Didn't you get my message? I had to work late."

"But your eyes, they're completely red. And there's . . . isn't that blood down your neck? And your hair . . . your shirt . . ."

How come I didn't notice that my eyes were bloodshot? Joe D. chided himself. And how could I have missed the blood on my neck?

"Are you all right?" asked Pamela. Joe D. looked at her—a tiny but very beautiful woman with long, lustrous black hair—and found himself unable to answer. It wasn't only that he couldn't decide if he was in fact all right or not. It was just that his lips wouldn't move.

"I think I'd better get you out of here," Alison said. "I'm sorry," she told her friends.

No problem, they said, clearly relieved, and recommended that Alison take Joe D. to an emergency room. Joe D. searched Alison's face for annoyance or anger and was gratified to detect only concern. "I love you, Alison," he said, and from the reaction of the others at the table he realized that this statement was viewed a bit strangely. "I do, I really do," he protested.

Alison stood up and helped him out of his chair. She held his elbow as they re-navigated the restaurant. Outside she found a cab and helped him into it. "Lenox Hill emergency room," she told the driver.

"No way," Joe D. said, and gave him their address.

"You need to see a doctor."

"I need to sleep."

"There's a huge lump on your head."

"Look, which is it?" the driver said.

Joe D. repeated their address, and Alison just collapsed back into the seat.

SEVENTEEN

It wasn't a restful night for Joe D. or Alison. She insisted on waking him every hour to make sure he didn't have a concussion. They'd been through this once before, when Joe D. had been brained on Fire Island, so Alison considered herself something of an expert. Joe D. told her that sleep deprivation would kill him faster than a concussion, but she was adamant, even setting the alarm every hour so that she didn't miss an opportunity to inflict torture.

By morning the lump felt a bit better and Joe D. was exhausted. Alison figured that he was out of the woods, having survived the night, and fell into a deep sleep.

Joe D. made a pot of coffee and drank most of it. Though the lump was less sore to the touch, his head still ached ferociously, as if he had a bad hangover, the kind that makes you swear off alcohol for good. The kind of hangover that makes suicide seem like an appealing remedy.

He retrieved the newspaper from the hallway and tried to

read it. But the words wouldn't sit still on the page. He thought about yesterday instead. Concentrating as hard as his stunned brain would allow, he pieced together the minutes leading up to his blackout. He'd found the checks made out to the Caribbean League. He remembered that the amounts were hefty, though he couldn't recall them exactly. He remembered turning over one of the checks to see who or what had endorsed it. That's all he remembered.

No, he'd seen something else. He closed his eyes to focus better, but a fireworks display appeared behind his eyelids. He opened his eyes. Words began to drift into his consciousness like skywriting, and evaporated just as quickly. "Trustee." He remembered that word, and grabbed a pen and a slip of paper to write it down. "Bank" had been on the back of that check too. He wrote it down. No other words floated by, so he got himself another cup of coffee, draining the pot. When he sat down he wrote the words "trustee" and "bank." Then, his hand seemingly acting on its own, he wrote "Cayman" beneath the two words. He didn't know where "Cayman" had come from—perhaps it had gone directly from his subconscious to his fingers—but, having written it, he knew he'd seen it on the back of the check last night.

Joe D. stared at the three words for a while. The check had clearly been cashed by a bank in the Cayman Islands. A trustee of some sort had endorsed it. Joe D. couldn't recall the actual signature, if there had been one. It might have been a stamp. Since the Cayman Islands are in the Caribbean, it didn't seem too unusual that the check had been cashed there. This was a bit disappointing. On the other hand, hadn't Arnot told Estelle Ferguson that the grants were for Caribbean-American arts activities? Didn't Caribbean-American mean Caribbeans living in the US? And Estelle had told him that she sent the checks to a New York City post office box. How did they get from there to the Cayman Islands?

He heard a noise from the bedroom and quickly made a

fresh pot of coffee, which was still dripping when a haggard-looking Alison emerged a few minutes later.

"How do you feel?" she said groggily.

"Better. You look like you could use another twelve hours of sleep, though."

"I feel like hell. Are concussions contagious?"

He wanted to talk about what he remembered from the day before, but held off. Under the best of circumstances Alison didn't enjoy conversation before at least one cup of high-octane coffee. She flipped through the *Times* while the coffee dripped. When it was done Joe D. brought her a cup. She seemed to inhale rather than drink. "What happened last night?"

He told her as much as he remembered, culminating in his morning discoveries. The story perked her up quite a bit. "The Caymans are known for great snorkeling," she said, and took a large dose of caffeine. "And banks."

"Banks?"

"Yeah. It's kind of like Switzerland. You can get a numbered account there, no questions asked. Good place for stashing money."

"So the Caribbean League could be just a shell for Arnot to use to take money out of the Art Alliance and into his own pocket."

She nodded. "The 'trustee' on the check was probably just someone at the bank authorized to cash and deposit the checks."

"How can I find out more about these checks?"

"You can't. That's why people go to the Caymans in the first place. The sailing's supposed to be good too, though I always get the Caymans mixed up with Tortola. One of them's known for sailing, the other for snorkeling."

Joe D. wasn't in the mood to discuss water sports. "It had to be Arnot that brained me yesterday. What I don't get is how he knew I'd be there."

"Maybe it's time to bring in the police."

Joe D. shook his head, a big mistake. He could feel his sore brain rattle against his skull. "The cops still think Samson's death was a random killing. And if I bring them in Franklin will fire me."

"How come?"

"He doesn't want publicity. And if he thought the police could help, he'd have gone to them in the first place."

"Then maybe you should think about resigning."

"What?"

"I don't like this."

"It's part of the deal, Alison. You're the one who wanted me to do this."

"I thought you'd be doing corporate work, not breaking into someone's office and getting the shit kicked out of you."

"If you wanted a lawyer or accountant . . ." He could sense an old, familiar argument surfacing, and stopped himself from getting in deeper.

"I want you. But I want you in one piece."

He could see tears forming around the edges of her eyes. "I'll be careful. But I can't back out now."

Alison nodded, almost imperceptibly. "I need a nap," she said, and left him for the bedroom.

Joe D. considered following her, but he'd had too much coffee to sleep now, and if Alison couldn't sleep either they'd end up continuing this discussion, which would add to his feeling of overall misery. Joe D. didn't particularly enjoy this part of his work either, the getting-hit-on-the-head part, but he also knew that for Alison it went deeper. She just didn't see herself living with a guy who breaks into buildings for a living. Her idea of investigations was discreet credit checks and maybe the occasional stakeout. Helping him get started in his own business encouraged her to believe that he'd joined her world of young Manhattan professionals. The lump on the back of his head showed her how false this notion really was.

All during the rest of the morning his head slowly cleared, like fog lifting from a damp field. He remembered that he'd done something else yesterday before breaking into the New York Art Alliance. He'd gone to visit Arthur Rudolph.

Joe D. found the piece of paper with Arthur Rudolph, Junior's name and telephone number. Maybe Arthur had contacted his son, or maybe Junior could fill Joe D. in on a few details about his father's relationship with George Samson. Joe D. punched in the number. After four rings he heard the click of an answering machine picking up. "Thank you for calling. I'm sorry I'm unable to take your call, but if you leave your name and number, I'll get back to you as soon as possible. Please wait for the beep."

The beep came and went. Joe D. left no message. In fact, he had to remind himself to hang up, so riveting did he find this admittedly boilerplate message. He waited a few moments, then redialed the number and listened to the message over again. The voice was definitely familiar. Deep, rich, cultivated. Whose voice? Joe D. had never spoken to Arthur Rudolph, Jr. before. Then why did this voice sound so . . .

Then he knew. He called the number a third time just to be sure. He listened to the recording, but what he really heard were several of the pieces in this puzzle clicking into place.

The voice belonged to Howard Lessing.

EIGHTEEN

Alison slept as Joe D. dressed. He left her a note saying he'd be back in a few hours and headed downtown for Joanna Freeling's loft. He figured Howard Lessing—make that Arthur Rudolph, Jr.—would be there. They had more than likely spent Saturday night together, and spending the night in his shoe box of an apartment would have been a physical near-impossibility.

He rang the buzzer in Joanna's grimy vestibule and waited, patiently this time, for her to make the journey from wherever she was in the vast loft to the intercom near the front door. "Yes," she said a few minutes later.

"It's Joe DiGregorio. I need to talk to Howard Lessing."

There was a long silence. He wondered if she were checking with Lessing or just deciding on her own whether to allow the interview to take place. Finally, the front door buzzed open.

Joe D. climbed the three flights and began to regret coming here. It wasn't only that his head throbbed with every step. It would have been far less cruel to confront Lessing alone, without Joanna present. Less cruel, that is, unless Joanna already knew that her boyfriend was the son of her uncle's archenemy. In any case, Joe D. couldn't wait until Monday to talk to Lessing. He needed to find out what was going on.

Joanna greeted him at the door wearing a floor-length red silk kimono. It was nice to see her in a color other than black. The robe accentuated her pale, delicate features and her long, slim figure. There was something very studied about the way Joanna looked. Joe D. guessed she never put on even a bathrobe without considering its effect on her appearance. "Follow me," was all she said, and led him on a eastward trek through her loft to a small sitting area he hadn't seen on his first visit. Lessing was lying on a sleek black couch. He was reading a newspaper but put it down when they approached. He was wearing a long white terry cloth robe. It looked freshly laundered.

"You don't have to be here," Joe D. told Joanna. "I need to talk to Howard."

"I have nothing better to do," she said slowly and rather ominously, Joe D. thought, as if she were auditioning this sentence as a subject of her next "painting."

Disappointed, Joe D. took a seat across from Lessing, who was still reclining. The chair was a piece of stiff black leather slung between a pair of bent chrome poles. It looked uncomfortable, and it was. Joanna remained standing, her arms crossed as if a cold breeze were blowing in from the western zone of her loft.

Joe D. quickly debated between a accusatory confrontation and a gentler, inquisitive approach. In deference to Joanna's presence he chose the latter. "Do you know anything about Arthur Rudolph?" he asked as innocently as he could.

Lessing immediately looked at Joanna, who looked back at him.

"I think you mean that question for me," she said. "He was a business associate of my uncle's. They both owned stores." She made owning stores sound like slaughtering chickens.

Joe D. stared straight at Lessing, who had started breathing heavily. After a few moments he sat up.

"He's my father," he said with some defiance.

Joanna raised a hand to her mouth.

"Please, Joanna, try to understand. If I had used my real name, Rudolph, Arthur Rudolph, you wouldn't have let me near you."

Lessing—Rudolph—seemed to think that this was all the explanation that was called for. He sat back and crossed his legs at the knee, adjusting his robe in the process.

Joanna lowered herself into a chair next to Joe D. She moved with arthritic slowness. Her lips parted but nothing emerged.

"Why did you want to meet Joanna?" Joe D. asked. "Revenge?"

Lessing-née-Rudolph started to rise from the sofa as if to attack Joe D. for making this accusation. Joe D. started to get up too, and when Rudolph saw this he fell back into the sofa. "I didn't *want* to meet Joanna. I simply met her."

"A coincidence?"

Joanna actually looked hopeful for a moment.

"Absolutely. We met at an opening."

"Do you go to many openings?"

Rudolph shrugged. "Some."

"The way you pursued me that night, I'd never felt so . . . desired."

Both men turned and stared at Joanna as if she'd awakened from a long coma.

"You never mentioned what you were doing there. You've never wanted to go to galleries since then." She was staring at Rudolph with amazement, almost as if she were impressed with the success of his deception, rather than injured by it.

"What did you want from her?" Joe D. asked.

"Okay, at first I thought about getting close to her because of her uncle. He ruined my father, and she was his only heir."

"You figured you could get your father's money back by, what, marrying her?"

Lessing/Rudolph looked at Joanna. "Maybe at first. Then I fell in love with you. Truly." There was no way to make these words sound other than syrupy and insincere, but he'd taken a pretty fair stab at it.

She turned away from him.

"Don't you think someone would have figured out who you really were?" Joe D. asked. "I mean, I don't think Samson would have left Joanna anything if he found out she had married Arthur Rudolph's son."

"Maybe. I hadn't really thought this through. You have to understand. All my life my father was this rich, powerful man. I grew up thinking I'd never have to worry about money. I was a writer, I figured I'd never make a living on my own. But I wouldn't have to. Then George Samson destroys my father and robs him of every last cent."

"Your father *spent* every last cent trying to get revenge," Joe D. corrected him.

Lessing/Rudolph ignored this. "When I read somewhere that Samson had a niece, I knew I had to get to know her. I didn't have a plan all worked out."

He was addressing these words to Joe D., as if Joanna wasn't even in the room. She was staring into space, as if in fact she weren't there. Then Joe D. spotted a single tear detach itself from Joanna's eye and shimmer down her pale cheek. It clung to the edge of her chin for a moment before plunging to her lap.

"Maybe I thought, unconsciously, that I could recover

some of my father's money by marrying her. But I never had a plan. I just needed to get close to her."

Joe D. found himself almost believing him. Lessing/Rudolph wasn't evil so much as weak. But in Joe D.'s experience, weak people were usually far more dangerous. "Where is your father?" Joe D. asked. He wanted this interview to be over as soon as possible.

"In a rest home. He lost his mind along with his money."

"He's not there now."

"Ah, so you know that too."

"Has he contacted you?"

Rudolph shook his head.

"When was the last time you spoke to your father?"

"A week ago. I call him every Sunday." His voice caught here. "He didn't always make a lot of sense. But I think he knew who I was."

"Was it you who sent him the clippings about George Samson?"

Rudolph looked momentarily surprised. "That's right. Samson was the only thing he was interested in. The idea of getting even with Samson kept him going." Rudolph's eyes widened momentarily, as if he'd realized the implication of what he'd said.

"Did he know about you and Joanna?"

They both looked at her, still staring blankly.

"Absolutely not."

Suddenly, Joanna came to life, almost startling Joe D. "Get out, both of you," she said with unexpected composure.

Joe D. was only too happy to obey. He'd learned what he'd needed to know. Joanna Freeling hadn't known who her boyfriend was, and wasn't, therefore, involved in some weird scheme to punish her uncle by marrying his enemy's son. And Arthur hadn't heard from his father.

Rudolph stood, crossed to Joanna, and took her hand. "Darling, you know that I love you."

"Just leave," she said evenly, without looking at him.

"You can't deny the past six weeks, what we've shared."

"Can't I?"

"Try to understand."

"I understand perfectly. Get out."

"I think you should do what she says," Joe D. told him. "Maybe later . . ."

Rudolph looked at her forlornly. He did seem to have genuine feelings for her. Or was the desperation in his eyes due to the loss of a potentially huge chunk of George Samson's money? There was no knowing.

Joe D. held Rudolph's arm as they descended the steep staircase from Joanna's loft. He seemed about to pitch forward.

"I should kill you," Rudolph said, but his voice was anything but violent.

"Sooner or later she'd have figured things out."

"I always knew that."

"Then why'd you stick around?"

Rudolph just shook his head. "I actually loved her. I mean, she's a spoiled thing, and those paintings . . ." He chuckled mirthlessly. "But I loved her. She's so full of herself, she's almost irresistible. And when Samson was killed, I started believing that things could work out."

"Samson's death was a good deal for you, then."

"It was a good deal for a lot of people. But I didn't kill him."

They'd reached the vestibule. Joe D. held open the front door for Rudolph, then followed him out to the sidewalk. "Did your father kill him?"

Rudolph turned angry. "He couldn't have. He was too deranged to plan something like that."

"Doesn't take much planning to jump into a cab and pull a trigger a couple of times."

Rudolph seemed momentarily fazed by this, though of course the thought that his father could have murdered Samson must have occurred to him already. "I told you, I haven't spoken to him since last week."

They walked a few blocks together, neither inclined to speak. "I'm going to get the subway here," Joe D. told him at Houston Street.

"I think I'll keep walking. Maybe I'll get lucky and a bus'll run me over."

It wasn't easy feeling sorry for a guy who's biggest problem was that he'd expected to inherit millions and then hadn't. Still, Joe D. found himself almost pitying Rudolph. "Call her later. You never know."

The words sounded hollow, even to Joe D. But he also knew that some women would forgive anything—getting slugged with a closed fist, being cheated on, watching their children being abused. Joanna Freeling didn't strike him as the forgiving type, let alone a masochist, and what Rudolph had done would take a Mother Teresa to forgive, but it was worth a shot. You just never know when women are involved. "I was once in your shoes," he found himself telling Rudolph, surprised to be confiding in him. "I got to know a woman under false pretenses, and she found out."

"What'd she do?"

"She threw every loose object she could get her hands on. Now we're living together."

Rudolph seemed to take some comfort from this. "If you find my father, let me know, okay? I can't stand the idea of him wandering around."

Joe D. promised he would, and the two men parted.

NINETEEN

Alison was dressed and reading the Sunday *Times* when Joe D. got back to the apartment. His head had resumed throbbing, and he was looking forward to a nap. Alison reminded him that they had made plans to visit her mother in Westchester.

This news was like a second blow to the head. It wasn't that he disliked Selma Rosen, or even that he knew she disapproved of him. No, it was her efforts to be cordial to him that made him miserable. She was constantly wincing and puckering and squinting when he was around, trying to disguise the fact that she found him lacking in every way—wrong profession, wrong religion, wrong address (Alison's). An afternoon with Selma made Joe D. long for a confrontation, and he wasn't much for confrontations. But an out-and-out argument is always easier to take than the feeling of being just barely tolerated.

Joe D. showered and changed and they took a cab down

to Grand Central, where they caught the local to Scarsdale. "You look like you're about to face a firing squad," Alison told him on the train.

He answered, "I wish."

Selma was standing on the platform of the Scarsdale Metro-North station. She was a tall, thin woman of sixty or so with salt-and-pepper hair who always reminded Joe D. of Geraldine Ferraro. Most of Alison's attractive features—her angular face, her pale blue eyes, her high forehead—came from Selma, though on the whole she resembled her father, who had the sharp, intelligent look that was Alison's single best quality. Selma was invariably well dressed, often overdressed. Today she looked a bit formal for a Sunday afternoon. She had on a white blouse, a fashionably short skirt, and a cardigan draped over her shoulders.

She kissed Alison and extended a limp hand for Joe D. "So nice to see you," she said through what could only be described as clenched teeth.

It was a five-minute drive from the station to Selma's house. This was the house Alison had grown up in; Selma had gotten it as part of her divorce settlement. Alison's father had left her for a much younger woman to whom he was now married. This woman's name was never uttered in Selma's presence. Alison's father, for that matter, was rarely mentioned either. Fortunately, though Alison was an only child, there were legions of aunts and uncles, cousins, and second cousins.

The house always reminded Joe D. of the Texas oil man who, when asked by his architect to describe the kind of house he had in mind, took out a twenty dollar bill and pointed to the engraving of the White House. The Rosen house wasn't quite as large as the White House, but it was almost as imposing; a big, white affair behind a row of columns and an expansive, perfectly cropped lawn. Like the White House, it was more symbol than home; it bespoke wealth and power and standards rigorously maintained rather than warmth, pleasure, or family spirit.

Selma drove them into the garage, opening the double door by remote control. Joe D. had never entered the house except through the garage. Alison told him not to take this personally; she'd only been through the front door once or twice herself, and certainly not in the last ten years.

Now what? Joe D. inevitably thought once they'd arrived chez Rosen. The three of them made such a small, uncomfortable group. He knew the women would have a much better, more relaxed time if he weren't there, but Alison always insisted he accompany her on her bimonthly visits. She figured that familiarity would breed acceptance. So far she'd been wrong.

They sat in the den, a large room off the center hallway that was somewhat less formal than the rest of the house, though it always reminded Joe D. of a set for a sitcom, with its forced homeyness. The two identical sofas were covered in a neutral tweed, separated by an oversized coffee table heaped with magazines and books. Above a never-used fireplace hung an oil portrait of Alison, aged sixteen. It was a stilted picture, not much more animated than a yearbook photo. Alison looked dreamy, almost distracted, her eyes glancing off to the side. On its own above the fireplace, the portrait always struck Joe D. as quite sad, a fitting remnant of a lonely childhood.

"Alison tells me you have a major new client," Selma said with what sounded like a stab at enthusiasm. He loved the way both women referred to his cases as "clients."

"Well, it's new."

"Alison says you're working on the Samson murder." She said "Samson murder" the way a caterer might say "Goldstein bar mitzvah."

He started to tell her about the case when she interrupted him. "Alison, remember Sumner and Elaine Farkas, from Larchmont?"

Alison's shrug was ignored.

"Well, Sumner was blouses. Very big. He did a lot of business with Samson Stores. And I'm positive he and Elaine used to socialize with the Samsons. In fact, I think Elaine and Mona were quite palsy-walsy."

One of Selma's favorite conversational gambits was making a connection between anyone mentioned, no matter how remote, and herself or one of her friends. You could mention the Sultan of Brunei, Joe D. believed, and she'd know someone who knew someone who had once sat next to him at the theatre.

The conversation shifted to the Farkases, migrated to a discussion of their enormously successful and tantalizingly unmarried son, Roger, and finally settled on a lengthy cataloging of recent marriages, divorces, separations, and affairs. Joe D. excused himself and left the room.

He needed a phone and decided to try a room on the second floor. He ascended the staircase that rivaled that of the New York Art Alliance's. Both edifices, he realized, shared a kind of imposing sterility that seemed impervious to human intervention. The second floor was bisected by a long, dark hallway, off which were untold bedrooms. Joe D. poked into several before discovering one with a telephone.

He had looked up Stuart Arnot's number before leaving New York. Once his mind cleared early that morning he concluded that it had to have been Arnot who'd knocked him out. Who else but Arnot knew what Joe D. was looking for in his office on Saturday? Whoever hit him had grabbed the bank statements—only Arnot would know precisely what documents to take. Joe D. was eager to know how Arnot had found out that he was going to be at the Alliance headquarters that day. Had Estelle Ferguson tipped him off in a last-minute fit of conscience? If not, was she perhaps in danger?

Joe D. dialed Arnot's number. After a few rings he heard a loud series of clicks. Then the phone resumed ringing, but with a different tone this time. A woman's voice answered.

"Arnot residence."

"Is Stuart Arnot in?"

"He's playing tennis. Shall I interrupt him?"

Joe D. wasn't aware of any backyard tennis courts in Manhattan. "Where am I calling?" he asked, feeling foolish.

"This is Mr. Arnot's house in Connecticut." She sounded a bit testy.

"But I dialed . . ."

"You were probably transferred automatically. Mr. Arnot has call forwarding. He activates it every Friday before he leaves for the country."

Oh, the wonders of modern technology. Then something occurred to him. "When did Mr. Arnot arrive in Connecticut this weekend?"

A long pause.

"It's just that I thought I saw Stuart yesterday evening in Manhattan," Joe D. lied.

"But that's impossible. He arrived Friday night about nine. Shall I get him?"

"Are you sure he arrived on Friday?"

"I made him a late supper."

"On Friday."

"The day before yesterday, correct." Now she was being patronizing.

"I could swear I saw Mr. Arnot in Manhattan on Saturday."

"It must have been someone else."

"Perhaps he drove back into the city yesterday afternoon."

"He was here all day. I made him lunch at one. He played tennis from about two to three-thirty with the Paulsons. They're his houseguests this weekend. Now, shall I interrupt his game?"

Joe D. processed this news. If Arnot was in Connecticut on Saturday he couldn't have been the person who knocked him out. He had three witnesses—the woman on the phone and the Paulsons—to prove it.

He considered speaking to Arnot. But what would he say to him? That he had broken into his office on Saturday? That he'd been knocked out while trying to steal some bank records that just might be incriminating? He decided he didn't need to speak to Arnot after all.

"Never mind. I'll call Mr. Arnot next week," he said, and hung up.

Alison and her mother were still talking about various friends and relations when he returned to the den. Alison was lying down on a couch, her head propped by a pillow. She looked comfortable in this house, which never failed to surprise Joe D. He couldn't imagine what it would be like growing up in a house like this, particularly as an only child. Alison had been in therapy for most of her adult life, a fact that still fazed him. (What do you talk about? he would ask her occasionally after her twice-a-week sessions. "Issues," she'd answer cryptically. Or, sometimes, "I'm working things out.") She'd once told him that as an only child she'd felt ignored rather than smothered. "I sometimes think that one child is easier to ignore than two or three. My parents were just too caught up in their own worlds to bother with me much, other than to make sure that I was properly dressed and looked after by a hired baby-sitter. Maybe if I'd had a brother or sister we would have formed a critical mass they couldn't have ignored."

Alison claimed that Selma started paying attention only after her husband walked out on her. "She started calling me every night, crying or screaming or just moaning. I felt like I was never really her daughter, and now all of a sudden I'm her mother." After the trauma of divorce abated, Selma restricted her calls to two or three a week, and Alison had fallen into a pattern of visiting once or twice a month. Joe D. didn't see why Alison felt she owed her mother even this much attention, if what she'd said about her childhood was true, but suggesting this to Alison was pointless: "I have to, that's all," she'd say, and then she'd usually leave the room.

But watching her lying comfortably on the couch, seemingly relaxed in a house that felt more like a hotel lobby than a home, Joe D. wondered if these visits weren't more than obligations for Alison. Perhaps she enjoyed the easy, familiar conversations with her mother, the more so because they were recent developments. Perhaps the place you grow up in is always your home, no matter how stuffy, no matter how unhappy the childhood. Perhaps Alison liked coming here because as an adult she could savor the attention she never got as a child.

Joe D. sat down across from Selma, who eyed him as if a stolen candlestick were poking out from his jacket. "Are you hungry?" she asked. "I could ask Bernadette to make you a sandwich." Her tone suggested that hunger was an animal trait with which she was only dimly familiar. Bernadette was Selma's latest housekeeper—she went through one or two a year. Bernadette lived somewhere in a warren of rooms above the kitchen and garage. Joe D. hadn't yet met her; at least he didn't think so.

Joe D. assured her he was not hungry.

"Are you sure?"

"Positive."

"I could easily have Bernadette make you something."

"No, really, I'm fine."

Selma sighed, as if Joe D. were being difficult. She was a woman of indomitable will and great resourcefulness who nevertheless felt that she wasn't quite up to the life she was living.

"Let's take a walk," Alison suggested.

Joe D. seconded the idea. Selma seemed about to demur, but Alison and Joe D. were already on their feet. She retrieved her cardigan from a closet in the front hallway, and they left the house through the garage.

* * *

On the train back to the city Joe D. told Alison about his call to Arnot.

"If it wasn't Arnot, who was it?" she asked.

"That's what I can't figure. But I do know that Samson's murder is connected to the New York Art Alliance. That's where he was coming from the night he was killed. What I don't know is what that connection is."

"Maybe Samson found out that Arnot was stealing money and Arnot had to kill him."

"But don't forget that Samson asked me to fake his murder just the day before. Why would he do that if he had information about a major fraud?"

The train sped through the dreary landscape of the South Bronx before racing through Harlem and plunging into the long tunnel under Park Avenue. The darkness surrounding them seemed to mirror their own thoughts, and they were quiet while the train sped south to Grand Central.

TWENTY

"Mr. DiGregorio? This is Mike Moran. From Mrs. Samson's building?" Moran was attempting to whisper, but his gruff voice was ill-suited to the task.

"I remember who you are." Joe D. had only just gotten dressed. It was 8:30 Monday morning.

"Our Mr. Williams? He's up there."

"With Mona Samson?"

"That's right. I come on at eight this morning, but the night man, he tipped me off that Williams and Mrs. S. came in together last night from the country. He never left."

A beep intruded on the line. Call waiting, a telephone feature which, like the answering machine, Joe D. always considered a mixed blessing. "Hold on, Mr. Moran." He depressed the switch hook and said "Hello."

"It's Estelle Ferguson."

Joe D. blinked as he momentarily shifted focus. "Estelle. Can I call you back?"

"I'm at a pay phone, on my way to the office."

"Hold on then." Joe D. switched back to Moran. "I'll be over in fifteen minutes," he told him. "I'll sit on a bench across from the building. When Williams leaves, take your hat off and fan yourself, okay?"

"Yes sir."

Joe D. switched to Estelle Ferguson. "I'm back."

"I just wanted to know how it went on Saturday."

Joe D. debated how much to tell her. "Did you mention to anyone else about our meeting?"

"Nobody. Why?"

"Because someone else was in the building on Saturday. Whoever it was knocked me out and took the bank records."

"Mr. Arnot . . ."

"He was in Connecticut all weekend."

"Oh my god," she said hoarsely.

"You're sure no one else knew I'd be in the building?"

"Positive."

"Okay. Your best bet is to act as if nothing unusual has happened. Just go about your job as always. If Stuart Arnot asks about the missing statements, which I don't think he will, say you know nothing about them, got it?"

"I hope I can act normally. I'm scared to death."

"I don't think you're in any danger. Whoever knocked me out didn't kill me. And you never saw those bank statements."

"Never."

"Then you're safe. Listen, does Arnot have a girlfriend?"

"Not that I know of. Why?"

"I have a feeling he may be planning to leave the country, and I doubt he's leaving alone. Those checks to the Caribbean League were deposited in a bank in the Cayman Islands."

"I usually make his travel arrangements."

"I don't think he'd have you book this flight. Has he mentioned a vacation or anything?"

"He usually spends his free time in the country. In fact, he's looking for a bigger place."

"In Connecticut?"

"That's right. He sold his current place and is looking for something larger in the same area."

"He sold the house he's in?"

"The closing is this afternoon, here in New York."

"Funny. Usually you buy a place first, then try to sell the one you're already in."

"Mr. Arnot said he got an offer for his house he couldn't refuse. A neighbor wanted to expand, something like that. So he sold it."

"How about the apartment in the city?"

"It's a rental."

Joe D.'s hunch that Arnot was leaving the country was looking solid. "Will you let me know if Arnot does anything that makes you think he's taking a trip?"

"Do you really think he's leaving?"

"I do."

"I'll call you, then."

"Good. And unless you need it, I'll keep the key to the Alliance building."

Joe D. stationed himself on a bench across Fifth Avenue from Mona Samson's building. The bench was low and concrete and, though it was a warm morning, it sent damp, cold waves up through his spine. It stood in front on a high stone wall that formed a barrier between Central Park and the sidewalk along Fifth. Mike Moran spotted him after a few minutes and nodded. Joe D. had brought along a paper, but kept it on his lap, afraid that he'd miss Williams.

An hour later, at 10:15, there was still no sign of Williams. Someone like Mona Samson probably slept till noon, Joe D. was thinking. Breakfast in bed, a long bath. Would Williams stay with her all morning?

It was an overcast day, and it was slowly beginning to deteriorate. Rain was a good possibility. Joe D. occupied the next few minutes worrying about this. He didn't fear getting wet so much as he worried that he'd look obvious sitting on a bench in the pouring rain, staring at an apartment building. Even the most deranged homeless took shelter in a storm.

People trickled out of the building all morning. Most of them were well-dressed women who got into waiting cars or had Moran hail them a cab. There were a few nannies pushing strollers. One or two men. Each time a man left, Joe D.'s heart began to race. Moran would look at him, as if guessing what he was going through, but he never removed his cap.

Finally, at about 11:30, a man who looked to be in his mid-thirties appeared. He stepped under the canopy and poked a hand, palm up, out from under it. Satisfied that it wasn't yet raining, he turned left and headed south. Joe D. stared at Moran as if willing his cap to lift from his head. Moran waited a moment; then he did in fact remove the hat, fanning himself as if overheated.

Joe D. jumped to his feet and headed downtown on the opposite side of Fifth Avenue from Williams. He trotted for a few minutes to catch up with Williams, then slowed to match his gait. At Seventy-second Williams turned left, heading east. Joe D. crossed Fifth and followed him to Madison, keeping a ten-yard distance. At Madison Williams turned right, and walked downtown for a few blocks. Just north of Sixty-ninth Street he entered a shop.

Joe D. walked past the shop. He managed to glance in the window and saw that it was an antiques store. He crossed the street, planning to watch the store from the other side of Madison. Then he noticed the name above the window. Kendall Williams, Fine Antiques. It looked like Williams was the owner, not a browser.

Joe D. recrossed Madison and entered the store. It was small and crowded and suffused with the pungent odor of furniture polish and money. Williams's taste ran to the ornate. Many of the pieces were gilded, and there were a lot of oversized mirrors and flamboyant chandeliers. A narrow path ran through this clutter. Joe D. tried to check the prices on a few pieces, but couldn't find any. There might as well have been a sign in front: "If you have to ask . . ."

At the back of the shop was the one piece of furniture that appeared to be in use. It was a small, intricately decorated antique desk of blond wood inlaid with a darker pattern. Behind it sat an elderly woman of slightly newer vintage. She looked to be about sixty or seventy, with a pouf of gray-blue hair girding a pleasant, pink face.

"May I help you?" she said in a tone as skeptical as it was gracious.

"I'm looking for Mr. Williams."

"You're in luck. He's just arrived. May I tell him who's asking for him?"

Joe D. handed her a card. She took it, studied it, glanced quizzically at Joe D., and then rose and knocked on a highly polished wood door behind the desk. She opened the door, slipped in, and closed the door behind her. A moment later she reappeared and told Joe D. he could go in.

Williams's office was tiny and windowless. But it was stuffed with what must have been a king's ransom of antiques. In fact, it was crowded with so much gilded furniture and bric-a-brac it reminded Joe D. of a photo he'd once seen of King Tut's tomb when it was discovered. The tomb had been crammed floor-to-ceiling with treasures in a frenzy of greed, just before it was sealed for what was hoped to be eternity, but turned out to be just a few thousand years. Williams's office had a similarly frantic aura to it, as if he were drawing about him as much loot as he could to ensure himself a kind of immortality.

"I'm Kendall Williams. Can I help you with something?" he said.

Williams hadn't gotten up when Joe D. entered his office, but Joe D. knew from following him that he was on the tall side. He was quite handsome, albeit in that over-processed way that Joe D. couldn't stand. His hair was impeccably cut and had obviously been painstakingly blow-dried that morning. He was tan, but it was a seamless, neon tan from a bottle. He was wearing a navy double-breasted blazer, a muted red tie, and gray trousers. His supple, highly polished loafers, visible under the antique table Williams used as a desk, looked as if they'd been fashioned from embryos.

Joe D. sat on a delicate, ebony-colored upholstered chair. He let his weight settle onto it gradually, afraid that it might collapse. "I've been looking into the George Samson murder."

Williams's determination not to respond in any visible way to this was as obvious as if he'd jumped to his feet and proclaimed his innocence. His face froze, his breathing slowed, his eyes narrowed almost imperceptibly.

"I'd like to ask you a few questions about your relationship with Mona Samson."

"What makes you think I have a *relationship* with Mrs. Samson?"

The truth might get Moran into trouble. "You can't keep anything a secret these days," he said blandly.

A long, slow release of breath, then: "I suppose not. But wasn't Samson murdered at random?"

"The police think so. I've been hired by Seymour Franklin to make sure." He was about to explain who Franklin was when Williams sniffed, "Franklin's been fired."

"But I haven't. Maybe you can tell me what you were doing the night Samson was killed."

"I was home."

"Alone?"

"That's right. Do I need an *alibi?*" Williams made *alibi* sound like something a child needs to be excused from school.

"So you don't have one."

"I was home alone. Sorry."

"How long have you been seeing Mona Samson?"

He hesitated, as if deciding whether to reply. "About three years. There was a charity auction. We had an instant rapport. Mona has a very refined taste in antiquities. I wish I could say the same of her late husband."

Joe D. guessed her refined taste hadn't come from Mississippi, and was tempted to ask if she'd acquired it along with her lockjaw accent. "Did Samson know about the two of you?"

"If he did, he never said anything."

"Now that he's gone . . ."

"Will we be getting married?" Williams interrupted, a clear note of sarcasm evident. "Possibly. I haven't proposed." He said this with a lift of his chin.

"Has Mona?"

"Proposed? She's only been widowed for a week. Give the woman a chance."

Joe D. was trying to picture Williams and Mona Samson in a sexual relationship. It was a picture that wouldn't develop. Through dieting and surgery, Mona Samson had shorn herself of any overt tokens of feminity—breasts, curves, soft edges. Williams was her male counterpart. There was nothing feminine about him, but nothing really masculine either. He was like the furniture with which he surrounded himself: Gilded, polished, but essentially untouchable.

"Is Mrs. Samson a customer of yours?"

"Does she support me? No. Does she buy an occasional *objet?* Yes. We've gone on buying trips to Paris and London together as well. She's got a lot of square footage to furnish, and I've acted as her informal consultant."

"Are you paid for these services?" Joe D. hadn't meant to pluralize the word. Williams flushed.

"She covered our expenses on these trips. Nothing more," he said icily.

"Did George Samson know about the trips?"

"Of course. He had to approve the expenditures, after all. French furniture was very expensive in the eighties. Today," he sighed, "today, it's another story."

"I guess it's all relative," Joe D. commiserated. "How long have you had the store?"

"Nearly three years."

"So you opened not long after meeting Mona Samson."

"That's correct."

"Did she help you out financially?"

"That's really no concern of yours."

"I'm just trying to get a picture of the people surrounding George Samson. He was a very rich man, and I'd like to know how many people were dependent on him, that's all."

Williams pounded a fist on the table, which Joe D. half expected to buckle under the impact. "I was never dependent on George Samson!"

"But on Mona?"

"Her either. True, she did lend me a bit of money to set up shop. You need an inventory to get started, two months' rent in advance, and on Madison Avenue that can be a fortune in its own right."

"Have you repaid her?"

He waited before answering. "Not yet."

Joe D. couldn't think of anything else to ask Williams, and the office was beginning to feel stifling. He stood and thanked him.

"If you ask me, the person you ought to be talking to is Joanna Freeling. Samson's niece. She's the one with the most to gain with him gone."

"That seems to be the general sentiment. Do you know her?"

"I've met her at a few parties. I'm sure she had no idea I was . . . well, who I am."

"You seem to dislike her quite a bit, considering how little you know her."

"She's a no-talent hypocrite," he said, displaying more emotion than at any time before. "She's the one with the real motive for killing Samson. Mona already had everything she needed. Why bother to kill Samson, when the real beneficiary would be that tart?"

A good question, and one that had occurred to Joe D. as well. As for answers, well, with Samson out of the way Williams was free to marry Mona. Even the income from her portion of the estate would pay for an awful lot of antiques.

TWENTY-ONE

It was time to stir up trouble. Joe D. reached this conclusion after returning, wet and cold, from his meeting with Williams. It had begun to rain while he was in the shop, a bone-numbing April storm that made New York, a city of pedestrians, almost uninhabitable. The light on his answering machine was steady as a lighthouse beacon, and he realized, after a warm shower, that he had no right to be disappointed. Who, after all, would be calling? Samson's murderer, to confess? No, the main players in this case were hunkering down, quite comfortably. Each had gained considerably from Samson's demise, whether or not it was a random hijacking. Mona was still filthy rich, and could begin to come out of the closet with her lover. Joanna Freeling was richer than ever, though perhaps a bit lonely at the moment. Howard Lessing, aka Arthur Rudolph, Jr., had the satisfaction of seeing his father's nemesis undone. And Stuart Arnot had five million stashed in a Caribbean bank, without the annoyance of having his organization's largest benefactor snooping around.

No, everyone seemed to be quite satisfied with the status quo, which is why Joe D. felt he had to stir things up.

He decided to start with Mona Samson.

Mike Moran was on duty when Joe D. returned to the Samson building at about 4:30. The clouds had retreated across the East River to Long Island, leaving Manhattan temporarily bright, with an all too rare rinsed-clean scent in the air that would doubtless vanish any moment.

Moran greeted him with a resolutely unforthcoming expression. "Mrs. Samson," Joe D. said.

"And whom may I ask is calling?" he asked without irony.

"Joseph DiGregorio."

Moran called up on the house phone, and then pointed Joe D. to the elevator without so much as a wink of recognition.

Like the first time they'd met, Mona Samson was in the library when Serena showed Joe D. in. He looked around and doubted if many of the books had been disturbed since his last visit. Nor had Mrs. Samson put on much weight during the past week; she still didn't make a dent in the plump couch on which she perched, without leaning back, like a marionette suspended from above by strings. She motioned for Joe D. to sit in a wing chair across from her.

"Still trying to make something out of my husband's murder, are you, Mr. DiGregorio?" She said his name through clenched teeth, as if pronouncing it physically pained her.

"I guess you already know I visited Kendall Williams?"

"He called about it."

"The fact that you have a lover puts a new slant on things."

"Does it? George had lovers too."

"Then you had a double reason to want him dead." Oooh, Joe D. was feeling real aggressive. Mona Samson, however, seemed impervious.

"Wanting someone dead and killing that person are two

quite different things." She reached in front of her and lifted a teacup from a saucer on the coffee table. The cup was so delicate Joe D. could see the liquid through the porcelain. She raised the cup to her lips but seemed to merely kiss it, rather than take an actual sip.

"Did your husband know about Williams?"

"Absolutely not. We were very discreet."

"Are you positive about this?"

"Quite. George wasn't exactly observant, except when it came to cheap women's sportswear. He could identify a swatch of polyester from a thousand feet, but I daresay he wouldn't have noticed Ken Williams if he caught us passionately embracing right here in this library."

Joe D. was tempted to ask in what in part of Mississippi they used words like *daresay*. "Did he ever meet Williams?"

"Once or twice. On the charity circuit."

"How serious is your relationship with Williams?"

She started to reach for the teacup but changed her mind and sat back. "How did Ken . . . Mr. Williams characterize it?"

Joe D. detected a hint of vulnerability in the question, the first visible crack in her composure. "He didn't say," he answered truthfully, though Williams had in fact seemed rather cavalier about his benefactress.

Mona seemed disappointed in his answer. "It's serious," she said.

"Will you two be getting married eventually?"

"Possibly," she said with what sounded to Joe D. like forced casualness.

"What was your involvement with the New York Art Alliance?"

"I was the wife of its largest benefactor."

"Nothing more direct?"

"I went to innumerable fund-raising dinners. I even chaired one or two of them. Why?"

"Did you have much to do with Stuart Arnot?"

"I met him at the dinners, of course. Why?"

"Your husband never mentioned any concerns about Arnot?"

"Concerns about what?"

"That Arnot might have been doing something improper with the money he handled."

"George never mentioned anything about it. Not that he would have," she added. "He wasn't one to gossip." She make this sound like a singular failure.

"Stealing money from a charity is more than gossip."

"I suppose, but George never mentioned anything about it."

This wasn't getting him very far. He decided to take a chance. "A few days before he died, your husband and I met."

She cocked her head in a not altogether spontaneous gesture. "Did you?"

"He asked me to kill him."

"Ah, so you're actually investigating your own crime!" She laughed, a surprisingly deep, guttural sound that caused her bony shoulders to quiver.

"He asked me to fake his killing. I refused."

"You're an honorable man, then. I assumed he offered you packets of money."

"A million dollars."

"Weren't you even tempted? That's a lot of money, I daresay." Her face, surgically tightened, barely moved when she spoke. Joe D. had the eerie impression that he was watching a ventriloquist at work, making sounds without moving a muscle. But where was the dummy?

"You're making a joke out of this. I think you know more than you're saying."

"Thinking is your prerogative."

The woman was an icicle. "Why would your husband have wanted to fake his own death?"

"You're sure it was George you met with?"

A question that had been haunting Joe D. since taking this case. "Positive," he lied.

"Then, no, I can't imagine why George would want to *fake* his own death. Assuming you're telling the truth. You've accused me of lying. Perhaps you're the one who's lying."

"I never said you were lying, Mrs. Samson. Only that you know more than you're saying."

"Have you met with my niece?" She said this so matter-of-factly it took Joe D. a moment to realize that she had changed the subject.

"I did. And I learned that the man she's been seeing is the son of Arthur Rudolph. Did you know that?"

This piece of news finally made an impression. "I don't believe it," she gasped. He saw an undulation in her loosely draped blouse. Joe D. found this small movement reassuring. "I knew she hated George, but I never thought . . ."

"I don't think she knew who her boyfriend really was."

"Oh, don't you believe it. She's a calculating thing."

"Did you know that Arthur Rudolph was missing from his nursing home?"

"No, how interesting."

"Did you know Rudolph?"

"I suppose we'd met a few times on the . . ."

"Don't tell me, on the charity circuit?"

"That's right, before my husband bought him out. His family was once very prominent, you know."

"I gather they lost their prominence along with their money."

She didn't appear to enjoy this remark. "Don't be such a cynic, Mr. DiGregorio. Anyway, I believe the last time I saw Arthur was at a closing dinner celebrating the acquisition. About five years ago."

"Arthur Rudolph's last hurrah."

"I suppose it was. He wasn't pleased that George converted his precious stores to Samson's I wouldn't have been pleased either. But it was absolutely asinine of him to waste all his money trying to get even. And now his son has taken up the cudgel by teaming up with Joanna." She seemed to find this notion delicious.

"But what would Joanna have to gain by teaming up with your husband's enemy?"

This appeared to baffle her, but she recovered quickly. "Don't trust her, Mr. DiGregorio. She profited most from George's death, don't forget that. She had nothing, now she has thirty-nine million."

"Thirty-nine?"

"The market was up last week. Hadn't you noticed?"

"A lot of people profited from your husband's death."

"It's a matter of degree. It's always a matter of degree."

TWENTY-TWO

Continuing his effort to stir things up, Joe D. left Mona Samson in her library and headed straight for Stuart Arnot's office. So far the effort had proved futile. Mona Samson was as easily stirred as a vat of hardened cement. Perhaps Arnot would be less rigid.

The front door of the Alliance building looked unmolested. Joe D. had checked this point before leaving the building on Saturday, but he wanted to reconfirm it today, with a clearer head. It looked like whoever hit him that day had a key to the place. Not to mention the access code.

Once again Joe D. was struck by the aura of self-satisfaction that permeated the New York Art Alliance. The receptionist didn't seem pleased to see him. Nor did any of the other, mostly female, employees who passed by him. He seemed to carry with him the odor of the REAL WORLD, a place where money was earned rather than donated, and spent, not granted.

Like Mike Moran, Estelle Ferguson pretended not to recognize Joe D. He didn't enjoy this part of detective work. On his last case with the Waterside police he'd had to masquerade as an accountant, of all things, and he'd hated every minute of it. As Estelle led him up the grand staircase to the second floor, Joe D. whispered that he wouldn't get her into any trouble with her boss. He hoped this was true.

Arnot said nothing as Joe D. crossed his office and sat in one of the chairs in front of his desk. He couldn't help glancing over at the locked cabinet before which he'd recently had his brain pulverized. He turned quickly away. It seemed almost unfair that the only evidence of the crime that had taken place here was a diminishing but still sore lump on the back of his head.

"I'm very busy," Arnot said petulantly by way of greeting. Once again Joe D. was struck by how overshadowed Arnot was by his large and opulent office. Even his clothes—a starched blue shirt with white collar, red silk tie topped by a gold-collar pin, and rich-looking charcoal-gray suit with a blue handkerchief ballooning out of the jacket pocket—seemed to detract from rather than enhance their occupant.

"I won't keep you, then. I've been doing a little digging into the finances of the New York Art Alliance." Joe D. watched Arnot closely for a reaction, but found none. "A lot of money has been earmarked for something called the Caribbean League. Mind telling me what that is?"

"First of all, it's none of your business what the Alliance does with its money. And second of all, the Caribbean League supports arts programs within the large community of Americans of Caribbean descent."

"Especially those from the Cayman Islands."

Arnot didn't miss a beat. "I don't believe there are many Americans from the Caymans, as a matter of fact."

"Then why has more than five million dollars been deposited in a bank in the Cayman Islands?"

"How did you find . . ." Arnot stopped himself. His hands

automatically neatened a small pile of papers on his blotter. "What the Caribbean League chooses to do with its funds before disbursing them is their concern."

"Come off it. That money is being diverted to numbered accounts."

Arnot stood up and removed his jacket, which he placed carefully on the back of his chair. In his shirtsleeves he looked surprisingly powerful. His face had a boyish inchoateness, but his body appeared lean and strong. "If I find you've been talking to any of our employees, I'm going to have to file a complaint with the police."

"I have a feeling you're not eager to bring in the cops. Anyway, I've been digging at the New York Department of State," Joe D. lied. "You'd be surprised, the information they have."

"Would I?"

Joe D. didn't want to get any deeper into this lie than he already was, so he took a chance and changed the subject. "But I do admit to breaking into your office this weekend."

"What?" Arnot looked genuinely shocked.

"You mean you didn't know?"

"I certainly didn't."

"It was quite busy in here this weekend. Someone clobbered me on the head before I got hold of what I was looking for."

Arnot fell back into his chair. "And what was that?" he asked dispiritedly.

"Bank statements."

"What would you want with bank statements?"

"The ones I was looking for would tie you to numbered accounts in the Cayman Islands."

"Yet you never found any statements."

"Someone else got to them first."

Arnot didn't respond to this.

"Aren't you even curious who it was?"

"I'm not sure I believe a word you're saying."

"Are the statements missing or aren't they?"

"I haven't checked lately," Arnot replied smoothly.

"Who besides you has keys to this building? And the code to the alarm system?"

"My secretary has keys, one or two of our senior grant administrators."

"Would you mind if I talked to them?"

"If you must," Arnot sighed. He seemed momentarily overwhelmed by the whole business.

"Be honest with me. Did you or didn't you know that I was in your office this weekend."

"How *would* I know?"

"You'd know if the other person here told you."

"Then I didn't know you were here. As I said before, I've half a mind to call the police."

"But the other half tells you not to involve them."

Arnot smiled grimly, picked up a pen, wrote something on a slip of paper, and handed it across his desk to Joe D., who had to stand up and reach for it. There were two names on it, both female. "These two people, and my secretary, whom you've met, have keys to the building."

"You wouldn't by any chance be planning to leave the country?"

"I travel occasionally on Alliance business."

"I'm talking about a permanent absence."

"What makes you ask?"

"Only that you sold your place in Connecticut and have five million stashed in the Caymans."

Arnot took a deep, fortifying breath. "You have no right to accuse me of anything. Now, I said I was busy. . . ." He grabbed a handful of papers from his desk, as if proving his point.

Joe D. briefly questioned the two women who had keys to the building. Both looked incapable of hammering a nail, much less pummeling Joe D.'s head. Neither had given or lent her key to anyone. And both talked to Joe D. with the forced politeness they probably used on panhandlers.

The answering machine was winking when Joe D. got back to the apartment. The first message was from Alison, suggesting they eat out that evening. The second message was from Arthur Rudolph, Jr., asking Joe D. to call him. Joe D. had to remind himself that Rudolph was the same person as Howard Lessing. He returned the calls in reverse order.

"I wanted to know if you'd heard anything from my father."

"I was going to ask you the same thing."

"Oh." A disappointed silence followed.

"Have you been in touch with Joanna?"

"I've left messages on her machine. I'd say it's over."

Joe D. reassured himself that he'd only expedited the inevitable unmasking of Lessing. "Do you have any photos of your father?"

"Sure, plenty."

"Any recent ones?"

"Not since he's been in the nursing home. His looks kind of went to hell these past few years."

"Put together the best ones you have, the ones that would help ID him now. I'll come by and get them in an hour or so."

He called Alison and told her he'd pick her up at the store at 7:00. Then he headed downtown.

TWENTY-THREE

"Chip" Rudolph looked like an animal in a zoo before they started building roomier cages. It was almost as if he'd grown since Joe D. had last seen him, and now threatened to burst the confines of his tiny apartment.

Even Rudolph seemed to realize that something had changed. "I know it looks kind of crowded here," he said apologetically, shortly after Joe D. got there. "Joanna had my things sent over, and I just haven't found the heart to put them away."

Finding the heart should be easy compared to finding the room, Joe D. thought. Several boxes, still taped shut, were stacked in the middle of the room. But it was more than just the clutter that made Rudolph seem so out of place. Everything about him declared that this was a man whose horizons had recently shrunk.

"Did you find some pictures of your father?"

Rudolph crossed his apartment in two giant steps and

retrieved a shoe box from a shelf above his desk. He rejoined Joe D. in the "living" portion of the cubicle and began fishing through the box. He came up with a dog-eared photo and stared at it for a few minutes before handing it to Joe D. "I never know what to feel looking at these pictures. Anger or pity."

"Anger at your father or George Samson?"

"Both, I guess. That's the hard part, resenting both of them. Samson screwed my father, but my father just couldn't walk away. He lost everything trying to get revenge."

Joe D. studied the picture. Rudolph, Sr. was a tall man, on the hefty side. His face was fleshy, with oversized features. He appeared to be posing in front of a store, probably one of his; he had a proprietary grin on his face.

"Not a very flattering picture," Rudolph said.

Joe D. doubted if photos of Rudolph, Sr. ever were. Cameras like bones and sharp angles. Rudolph's father had neither.

"How old is this picture?"

"About five years. He's standing in front of one of his stores. A few months later he sold the chain to Samson and was booted out."

Joe D. squinted at the shot, held it at arm's length, then peered at it closely. "Can I keep this?"

"If it helps you find my father, by all means."

Joe D. stood up to leave. The tiny apartment forced an uncomfortable intimacy upon its occupants. Joe D. thought it best to keep his distance, and figured that the only way to insure this was to leave. Rudolph, still seated, started to speak, and Joe D. knew he wasn't going to get off easily.

"I don't know," he began. The words escaped his lips in a sigh. "I just don't know how to convince Joanna that I really love her."

"You may not be able to."

Rudolph looked at him as if he'd been given a death sentence. "But I do," he wailed.

"Then keep trying." Joe D.'s right hand was on the Medeco lock on Rudolph's front (and only) door.

"She thinks I only wanted money. Or revenge." Rudolph laughed ruefully. Joe D. struggled with a second lock, having broken one of his cardinal rules since moving to Manhattan: Never attempt to unlock someone else's door.

"The funny thing is, she and her uncle weren't even getting along. He kept threatening to disinherit her. If I was after Samson's money, I might have been barking up the wrong tree."

Joe D. abandoned the locks.

"You say Samson threatened to cut her off?"

"All the time. He couldn't stand the way she looked down on him. He'd invite her to one of his fund-raising dinners and she'd always find an excuse not to go. Or if she went she'd just sit there with her nose up in the air. Samson wasn't *cultured* enough for her. And he certainly never understood what her art was all about."

"Sounds like she was risking losing a lot of money."

"Joanna never truly believed he'd cut her off. I think she enjoyed thumbing her nose at Samson. And if things ever got too strained between them, she'd always make it up in some way. But lately things were worse than usual."

"How so?"

"He'd stopped asking her to things. This past winter, he never even invited her to his Christmas party. She'd call, and he wouldn't return her calls. Or he'd return them a week later, and act cold towards her."

"What was happening?"

"Joanna figured it was Mona's doing. Much as she hated her uncle's coarseness, she detested Mona's pretentiousness. And the feelings were mutual. During one of their reconciliations a few years ago Joanna gave her uncle one of her paintings. I think it was *Do not fold, spindle, or mutilate.*" Rudolph smiled and shrugged. "Anyway, the paintings were important to her. And she later found out that Mona had hung it in one of the servant's rooms in their Connecticut house."

Joe D. felt a pang of sympathy for the servant. "Do you think Samson might really have been planning to disinherit her?"

"Who knows?"

"Did Joanna *think* he was?"

"She was worried, let's put it that way."

"Worried enough to kill him before he did anything about it?"

Rudolph looked at him for a bit. "Didn't I already tell you that she was with me all night?"

"She could have hired someone." Or you could have done it together, he added silently.

Rudolph nodded.

"Was she with you that night?"

Rudolph answered in a slow, measured tone. "In the same loft, yes."

"That's kind of like saying you were both in Macy's at the same time. Are you sure she never left that night?"

"I was watching the Knicks on television. She was in her studio."

This wasn't really an answer. "She could have left the loft for an hour, couldn't she? And you'd never have known."

Rudolph just looked at him.

"For that matter, you could have left the TV on and slipped out yourself."

Joe D. could practically feel Rudolph's hot breath on his face. "Deep down, *here,"* Rudolph put a fist to his heart, "I know she didn't kill him."

"Did she own a gun?"

The fist left the heart and he nodded. "She was terrified of being alone in that huge loft." He couldn't resist looking around his own apartment, where hand-to-hand combat, rather than a gun, seemed the appropriate form of self-defense.

"Do you know what kind of gun?"

Rudolph shook his head. "What I just told you, about Joanna's troubles with her uncle? If she finds out I spoke to you about this, she'll never speak to me again."

"I won't let on who told me."

Rudolph looked so relieved it was almost touching. "You want to help me with these locks?" Joe D. asked.

Rudolph hesitated before pulling himself up. He seemed reluctant to end the conversation. "I've lost the woman I love and my father, both in the same week," he said. "Anything you can do . . ."

He seemed unable to complete the sentence. "I'll do my best," Joe D. assured him. He ran down the three flights and out onto the sidewalk, where he took a deep breath. Never had New York City air tasted sweeter.

TWENTY-FOUR

Joe D. walked to the corner of Seventh Avenue, and paused to figure out the quickest way to get to Joanna Freeling's. The southern end of Manhattan displayed none of the orderly grid-logic of the rest of Manhattan. He figured there probably was a bus connecting the Village with Soho, but he hadn't a clue where to get it. A cab would be faster anyway, he concluded, and stepped off the curb to hail one. It was close to rush hour, however, and as if that weren't bad enough, a slight drizzle had begun, both of which made finding an empty cab a long shot. As always in Manhattan, walking turned out to be the only completely reliable mode of transportation.

He walked quickly, zigzagging the intersections to avoid the red lights, and arrived at Joanna's building fifteen minutes later. The drizzle had intensified into a downpour. Raindrops cascaded from his hair like sweat. He wiped them away and buzzed her loft. He caught his reflection in the glass that covered the tenant list, and tried to make himself look presentable. The effort was futile.

Joanna greeted him at the door wearing a long black turtleneck over black leggings. She maneuvered herself to within inches of Joe D., looking up into his face with large, sparkling eyes. He couldn't decide if she was being seductive, or if she was one of those people who just weren't sensitive to physical distances between people. He took a step back.

"I hate this time of day, don't you?" she told him, and took a step towards him. She made this statement as if it were self-evident. When Joe D. didn't respond, she added some explanation, sounding a bit peevish. "Do you continue working, or knock off? Is it too early for a drink, or has the cocktail hour begun? It's an occupational hazard of the artist's life that you never know when to quit. I imagine people with office jobs know precisely when to quit." She made *people with office jobs* sound like a remote species. "But artists?" She waved both hands artistically.

"I have a few more questions about your relationship with your uncle," Joe D. said.

"More questions? Then let's have a drink."

She led him to the kitchen area of the loft, which Joe D. hadn't yet visited. It was an enormous, gleaming space. Tiles, countertops, appliances—all were shiny white and impeccably clean. It was either fashionably uncluttered or starkly institutional, depending on how you felt about ultramodern design. Joe D. found himself clenching and unclenching his fist; Joanna's kitchen reminded him of a blood donor center.

"I'm having Chardonnay," Joanna said. "And you?"

She was treating his visit as a social call, and he was tempted to decline a drink in the interests of professionalism. But the rain had chilled him and he felt he could use some fortification for the interview to come. He really wanted a beer, but was afraid it would clash with the decor. "Chardonnay's fine."

She removed a bottle from a nearly empty refrigerator

disguised as a cabinet. "I'm afraid I haven't anything to offer you in the way of hors d'oeuvres."

"No problem."

"I'm a vegetarian, you see," she offered pointlessly.

"You probably brake for animals too," Joe D. muttered.

"Sorry?"

"Nothing." In his experience, people became vegetarians more to express antisocial sentiments than pro-animal feelings. Joanna seemed no exception.

"I've been doing some digging," he began, once they were seated with their wine. "I've learned that you and your uncle were not getting along when he died."

"You've been talking to Howard," she said bitterly. Her tight black leggings accentuated the remarkable length and shape of her legs. "Or should I say Arthur." She waited a beat, then added, *"Junior."*

Her tone was so acid, Joe D. felt obliged to put in a plug for Arthur. "He's known as Chip, actually. And he really loves you, you know."

"Bullshit."

The word sounded especially lurid coming from Joanna's pale, delicate lips.

"Anyway, did you believe your uncle was planning to change his will before he died?"

"Uncle George and I never discussed *wills."* Her nose crinkled at the word. "Our disagreements, such as they were, weren't *about* money."

"What were they about."

"Art!" she said, as if this were obvious.

"The painting you gave him, the one he hung in his servants' quarters."

"Mona put it there," she spat, then inhaled deeply. "It was one of my best pieces. I worked for weeks on it."

Joe D. pictured her stenciling "Do not fold, spindle, or mutilate" a hundred times on a white canvas. If she did kill her uncle, an insanity plea would probably stick; she'd only have to bring her canvases to court to prove it.

"But if you think I murdered my uncle because he and his wife failed to appreciate my art, you're mistaken."

"But this episode did lead to a falling out, am I correct?"

"We had words."

"Did he threaten to disinherit you?"

She smiled coyly. "I'd hardly tell you if he had, now would I?"

"The night your uncle was killed, you and Howard—I mean Arthur—were here in the loft."

"As I told you last week."

"What were you doing?"

"Reading, I suppose."

"Both of you?"

"Chip may have been watching the television," she said, sounding annoyed. "He liked to watch television." She made this sound like a character defect on the order of pyromania.

"In fact, Chip told me he *was* watching TV. Mind if you show me where the TV is?"

She put down her glass and took him through yards and yards of loft until they reached her bedroom. A king-size bed covered in a bright quilt dominated the room. One wall was lined with floor-to-ceiling bookshelves filled with art books. There was even a library stand on wheels to reach the books on the top shelves. In front of the bed was a large television. Funny place for a person who never watches television to put a set, he thought.

"This your only set?"

"Yes."

"And where were you while Howard was watching?"

"With him on the bed."

"He was watching a basketball game."

"I could be a fan, you know."

"You could be, but Howard told me you were painting." If Rudolph ever had a chance with her, Joe D. thought, he'd dead in the water now. "Your studio's practically in another time zone from the bedroom."

"Very funny."

"But you could easily have slipped out for an hour and Howard would never have noticed."

"He could have slipped out too."

"Did he?"

"I don't think so. But he certainly had a motive for wanting George Samson dead."

"Oh?"

"Don't play dumb. My uncle destroyed his father. I don't think . . . Chip ever thought he'd have to earn a living. Now he's broke. He's bright enough to support himself somehow. He's got the credentials—Choate, Harvard. And I suppose some of his family's connections must still be worth something, even if the money's gone. He's just unmotivated."

"He writes," Joe D. offered in his defense.

"That's his *pretext,* his cover. It gives him something to talk about at cocktail parties. He has no dedication at all. And believe me," she added smugly, "dedication's what it takes."

That and a trust fund, Joe D. was tempted to add. He felt a surprising sympathy for Rudolph, and decided to steer the conversation away from Joanna's character assassination. "If Arthur was in here, and you were painting, then you can't be positive that he stayed in all night."

"I thought I was, but I suppose you're right. He could have left without my hearing him."

"Which means that you could have done the same."

"Touché."

"Do you own a gun?" He knew the answer, but didn't want to further implicate Rudolph.

"Oh, this is getting serious."

"Do you?"

She nodded.

"Mind if I take a look at it?"

"I don't have to show it to you."

Joe D. just shrugged. After a moment's pause she crossed the bedroom, opened a drawer in a small night table, and removed a pistol.

It was a Colt semiautomatic, the same type of gun used to kill Samson. True, it was the most common privately owned gun in the country, but a ballistics expert might be able to tie it to the murders through the cylinder markings on the bullets found in Samson and the driver. A sniff test told him it had been used recently.

"When did you last fire this?"

"A few days ago. I take lessons at a rifle club."

Funny sport for a vegetarian, he thought. "Are you afraid of someone?"

"Everyone in New York should be afraid. But I'm a very wealthy woman, as you know. And I live alone."

"May I borrow it for a few days?" Joe D. had a contact in the city ballistics department who could run a quick check for him.

"Absolutely not. I don't have to give it to you. And I don't want to be without protection even for one night."

"If the gun doesn't match the one used to kill your uncle, it would clear you."

"I don't need to be *cleared.* And certainly not by you. You're not even a cop."

She replaced the gun by her bedside and escorted Joe D. due east toward the living area. She sat down and picked up her wine, but Joe D. remained standing. He was trying to decide whether Joanna's refusal to give him the gun signified anything. If the gun had been used to kill Samson, she naturally wouldn't lend it to him—but then she'd hardly keep it by her bedside, either, if it was the murder weapon. On the other hand, she had a petulant streak. Joe D. had no doubt that she'd withhold the gun just to be difficult.

"It looks like you don't have much of an alibi anymore," he told her. "And you have a prime motive."

"I told you, it's not *about* money."

"I never said it was."

"Anyway, you're a private detective. I don't need an alibi for you. As far as I know, the police still think my uncle was a random victim."

The truth of this statement took the wind out of Joe D.'s sails momentarily.

"The person you should be harassing is Mona Samson," she said bitterly. "Talk about motive."

"What motives *are* we talking about?"

"She hated him. He wasn't *cultured* enough for her. All he could do was make money. He wasn't exactly a sweetheart, either. And he fooled around."

"She seemed happy enough with the arrangement they had."

"Don't believe it. She detested him and he hated her. It wouldn't surprise me to learn that he was planning on divorcing her."

Or faking his own death to get away from her. "If you think of anything else you want to tell me, you know where to reach me."

Joe D. left her in the living area and hoped he remembered how to find the front door. He regretted not leaving a trail of crumbs.

TWENTY-FIVE

Joe D. hesitated before knocking on the locked door of Many Fetes. It was just after 7:00. Inside he could see Alison straightening up the store. She replaced some items on the racks, refreshed a few displays. He enjoyed watching her work. She looked beautiful in a tight-fitting black suit from the store that wasn't the least bit corporate. She also looked happy in the store, and Alison had one of those faces that improves immeasurably with happiness, and falls to pieces when sad. A pout could look attractive on some women. On Alison a pout fell like a dark shadow across her face, obscuring its best features.

He knocked on the door after a few minutes. She turned, about to announce that the store was closed, and smiled broadly when she recognized him.

"I'll just be a minute," she said after unlocking the door. She finished tidying up while Joe D. browsed through the racks. Alison had great taste in clothes—the store had even gotten a small write-up in *New York* magazine—but some of the outfits he looked at were pretty bizarre. He held up a few and wondered how a woman could figure out how to put them on. "This one looks like a parachute vest," he said of one outfit, in pale beige, with an assortment of randomly placed holes and hefty brass hardware, and a price tag of $750. Alison frowned when she saw what he was referring to. "I think that was one of my mistakes. I'm marking it down next week." He considered suggesting a 110 percent markdown—the store plays seventy-five dollars to anyone who takes the thing off its hands—but thought better of it. Alison took her work personally, and that included her inventory. Hadn't *New York* referred to Many Fetes's "highly eclectic, very personal assortment of dressing-up dresses"?

They had dinner at a tiny Italian restaurant on a side street that Joe D. had passed several times recently on his nightly rambles. He'd thought it looked charming and out-of-the-way. After waiting twenty-five minutes for a table, he changed his opinion. Alison insisted they stay once she'd gotten a look at the place. "This is my market," she said, surveying the small but well-heeled crowd. "I want food, not market research," Joe D. protested, but to no avail.

They were shown to a table within swinging distance of the kitchen door. Alison ordered a glass of white wine and Joe D. had a beer. Their waiter handed them menus and recited the daily specials. The dishes *sounded* Italian, but Joe D. doubted his mother, a native of Naples, would have heard of any of them. That he'd heard of one or two of them was due solely to his relationship with Alison, who'd proven to him that there was Italian food that didn't come covered with red sauce. He was learning to enjoy things like carpaccio and radicchio and carbonara, but couldn't help pining for the old-style southern Italian food he had grown up on.

He filled Alison in on his day, grateful, after months of relative idleness, that he had something to tell her. "Why the photo of Rudolph?" she asked him.

"I have this hunch. What if it was Rudolph in the back of the limo, pretending to be Samson. I never got a good look at the guy, and Rudolph and Samson look enough alike that I could have been fooled."

"Is Rudolph sane enough to pull something like that off?"

"By all acounts, no. But I have another theory."

He paused to take a sip of beer when someone caught his eye. Across the small restaurant he saw a familiar face. Kendall Williams was engaged in what looked like an intimate conversation with a woman who appeared to be no older than twenty-five, thirty max. She was stunning, with straight dark hair, turgid lips, and a long, sculpted face. Both she and Williams were leaning over the table, eyes locked.

"What's the matter?" Alison asked.

"Don't turn around. . . ." Alison swiveled anyway and then turned back. "Thanks. Did you notice the guy at the table against the wall, with the stunning woman with the long straight hair?"

"You mean the handsome guy with Natalie Danielli?"

"Who?"

"Natalie Danielli. She's a model. I can't believe I missed her on the way in."

"You know her?"

"No, silly. But I've seen her in magazines. She's one of the top models. Who's the guy?"

Joe D. told her. "She's an improvement over Mona Samson."

"She's more attractive, you mean. There are other qualities, you know."

"Right. Mona Samson's richer."

"I wasn't thinking of money."

"Personality? Mona's refined her personality to the point of extinction."

"She seems so elegant in all the articles about her."

"Mona Samson is a piece of sand irritated into a pearl.

She's hard and glossy and dead." Joe D. glanced over at Natalie Danielli, a vision of life itself.

From where they were sitting there was little chance of Williams spotting them. Their waiter seemed to have lost them too, having disappeared after taking their orders. Joe D. decided to make sure that Williams saw him. He figured having something to hold over Williams's head might come in handy. He left Alison with her wine and walked over to Williams's table.

"Didn't we meet the other day?" he asked.

Williams waited a beat before unlocking his eyes from his companion. His face dropped when he saw who was standing over them. "Oh, it's you."

"That's right, Joe DiGregorio." He offered his hand to Natalie Danielli. "And you are . . ."

"This is Natalie Danielli," Williams drawled.

Joe D. shook her hand. "Pleased to meet you. Kendall and I have a mutual friend, don't we?"

"It's one thing to follow me to my store," he hissed. "But following me to a restaurant . . ."

Joe D. decided to let Williams think what he wanted. "How's the food?"

Williams just glared, but his date began to wax poetic about the veal *tonato* in a heavily accented voice that enhanced her credibility in the Italian food department.

"Thanks for the recommendation. And nice meeting you." Joe D. looked pointedly at Williams and returned to Alison. Miraculously, their dinners had appeared and, equally miraculously, he'd ordered veal *tonato.* One bite told him that Natalie Danielli's taste in Italian food was probably a sight better than her taste in men.

Williams and his date left soon afterwards, somewhat hurriedly, Joe D. thought. A number of heads, male and female, turned to follow Natalie Danielli's exit. Joe D. was surprised that Williams would risk Mona's wrath by dining in public with someone like Natalie, who was apparently well-known and would attract attention even if she weren't. He'd detected a trace of genuine feeling for Williams in Mona. Now it appeared her feelings weren't reciprocated.

He and Alison shared a *tiramisu,* another Italian food his mother had probably never heard of, and later walked it off with a detour through Carl Shurz park. The rain had cleared, leaving the night air heavy and damp. He put his arm around her shoulders, she put her arm around his waist. "I've never enjoyed walking like this until I met you," Alison said. "It always felt awkward."

"I guess we fit perfectly."

"Then opposites must attract."

He didn't respond to this but he thought about it. Were they really opposites? Did the fact that she was Jewish and he Catholic make them opposites? She'd gone to college, he hadn't. She had a "career," he was happy just to be able to pay the bills. Still, under all the differences he felt a strong similarity. It had something to do with an instinctive wariness of the world, and also to do with a never-ending feeling of dissatisfaction, as if true contentment lay just over an always receding horizon. Not the strongest of foundations on which to build a relationship, but at times like this, feeling close and safe together, it seemed sufficient.

The light on Joe D.'s answering machine was flashing when they got home. "Leave it for tomorrow morning," Alison told him. She went straight into the bedroom and started to undress. Joe D. fetched a glass of water from the kitchen and couldn't pass the blinking machine without pressing the "play" button. "Traitor!" Alison called as the machine rewound. "Workaholic!"

He shouldn't have bothered. His messages amounted to a series of beeps followed by dial tones, indicating several hangups. He reset the machine and joined Alison in the bedroom. She was already under the covers and looked inviting as hell. He was unbuttoning his shirt when the phone rang.

"Let the machine take it," Alison ordered, and this time he obeyed.

He was naked by the time the caller left a message. "It's Kendall Williams. I called a few times earlier. I have some information you might find interesting. I'm willing to share it with you. . . ."

Joe D. ran to the living room and picked up the phone. The answering machine screeched in his ear before he had a chance to disengage it. "Don't hang up!" he shouted into the phone. "It's me, Joe D."

"As I was saying . . ." Williams sounded hushed and conspiratorial. Joe D. guessed Signorina Danielli wasn't far away. "I have some information you might find interesting. I'm willing to share it with you on one condition."

Joe D. guessed what that condition was, and knew right away he'd meet it. "Shoot."

"First the condition. You'll never breathe of word about tonight to anyone."

"I'm like you; I like to keep a good restaurant a secret."

"Very funny. You know what I mean. I don't want Mona Samson to find out that I was having dinner with another woman."

Another woman struck Joe D. as an odd way to describe Natalie Danielli. Compared to Mona Samson she was another species. "Mum's the word."

"We're just friends, anyway. But Mona can be jealous. . . ."

"If you're just friends . . ."

"Do I have your word?"

"You do, assuming what you have for me is worth it."

"Oh, it is. You mentioned yesterday that you were looking for George Samson's secret lover?"

Joe D. felt his heart accelerate. "That's right."

"Well, I think I can help you find out who it is."

Williams, though still whispering, sounded odiously like a grade school snitch. "And?"

"Mind you, I didn't say I know who it is. Just that I can help you find out."

Williams paused to let Joe D. beg. "And?"

"Well, let's just leave it at *cherchez l'homme.*"

"Who?"

"Cherchez l'homme. A man. Samson was queer."

Joe D. let this sink in. "Gay?"

"Call it what you will. He liked men. Mona claims they haven't had sex since the first year of their marriage. Even then it was just the obligatory old college try, according to her."

Joe D.'s mind was frantically trying to recast the entire case in light of this news. "Who was his lover?" he managed.

"I haven't a clue. I just know that looking for girlfriends is a waste of time."

Joe D. was thinking that he knew where to start the search for Samson's lover.

Williams apparently found Joe D.'s silence unnerving. "So, we have a deal, right?"

"Deal?"

"Not a word to Mona about tonight. As agreed."

"Oh, yeah, right. No problem."

TWENTY-SIX

There was a knock at the door. Joe D. checked the clock by the bed and saw that it was just past 5:00 A.M. Feeling surprisingly alert, he got out of bed and answered the door. Only when it was too late, when the door was swinging open, did he realize that he hadn't put any clothes on. *Joe DiGregorio?* said one of the two men at the door. Both were wearing trench coats and both, strangely enough, reminded him of his father, who had died several years ago. *You're under arrest.* He knew right away what they meant. But he played dumb anyway. *For the murder of George Samson* said the other cop. *And some other killings we'd like to talk to you about.* Joe D. had been dreading the knock at the door, but, facing the two men now, he felt only relief at finally confronting the inevitable. It was only when Alison entered the living room, wearing a bathrobe, that he began to feel panic. *Joe D., who are these men? Why are you naked?* He turned and tried to explain. But he couldn't get beyond the first few words, which, every time he started, led him to a conclusion he didn't want to reach.

He awoke to one of those limbo states in which dream and reality compete for the mind's commitment. Reality won, but only after a good struggle. Even ten minutes later, in the shower, Joe D. felt an uncomfortable mantle of guilt oppressing him.

"Why so quiet this morning?" Alison asked as he drank his coffee. One of the mixed blessings of living with someone, or at any rate, of living with Alison, was having his moods and emotions scrutinized in painstaking detail.

"I had the strangest dream," he told her.

"Really?" She sounded eager, as she always was, to hear his dream. Alison had been in therapy for most of her adult life and saved her dreams the way some people collect souvenirs. Many a morning he'd find her scribbling madly on a small pad of paper, trying to nail down a dream before its inevitable evaporation. She also enjoyed "working on," as she put it, Joe D.'s occasional reveries.

"In the dream, I'm the one who killed George Samson."

She emitted a judicial "ummm."

"And I was naked when they arrested me."

He really wasn't in the mood to analyze the dream, but he knew there was no going back. "Guilt," she pronounced after a brief silence. "You feel responsible for something or someone."

"But Samson's dead, and the only thing I know for sure about this case is that I didn't kill him."

"In what way do you feel 'exposed' by this case?"

"Exposed?"

"Vulnerable. *Naked.*"

He hated this kind of discussion. "It's my first big case," he said dutifully. "So naturally I want it to turn out right."

"And you're afraid it won't," Alison said with satisfaction. "So the dream is really about feeling responsible not so much for Samson's death, but for solving the mystery of his death.

And the naked part has to do with feeling vulnerable on your first big challenge."

Accurate, he thought, but hardly earth-shattering. "Thanks for the analysis. I'm on my way." He kissed Alison and left her at the dining table. It was the first time he'd ever left the apartment on a weekday before Alison, and it felt as if he were breaking a fundamental law of nature.

It was early, just past 7:00, so Joe D. had no trouble getting a cab. He gave the driver Stuart Arnot's address, and then sat back and tried to forget what he was about to do. Traffic was mercifully light. Joe D. hadn't been out this early since moving to the city. Manhattan felt completely different at this hour, far more peaceful, even, than at 3:00 in the morning, when empty sidewalks still couldn't disguise the activity simmering behind apartment walls. Now, at 7:15, the city felt hushed, expectant, as if everyone were waking up after a tough night and speaking in soft voices.

Arnot was wearing a silk paisley bathrobe when he answered the door. Since Joe D. had been announced by the doorman, Arnot didn't look so much surprised as annoyed. "Couldn't this have waited until I got to my office?"

"I had this strange idea that you might be skipping town. I was worried you'd call in sick today, and maybe the rest of your life."

"That's absurd."

"What I need to talk about is your relationship with George Samson."

"Surely we've been over this before."

"He was your lover, wasn't he?"

Arnot's face froze, but he managed to move away from the front door and let Joe D. enter.

Arnot's apartment was small, but had been decorated in defiance of this fact. The walls were painted a dark, glossy green. An oversized sofa dominated one wall. Facing it was a cluster of mismatched chairs upholstered in a rainbow of fabrics. An oriental rug covered most of the floor. Piles of big art books sprouted on top of the coffee table, under the coffee table, in corners. Extravagantly colorful fresh flowers were stuffed in vases all over the room. It was the kind of place that made Joe D. feel like a kid, afraid he'd knock over or spill something.

Joe D. cleared a clump of throw pillows from one section of the couch and sat down. Arnot selected a chair opposite him. "How did you find out?"

"You can't keep this kind of thing secret forever."

"But we did. We did."

"How long were you and Samson lovers?"

Arnot hesitated. "I'm not used to talking about this. Forgive me." Another pause, then, "Almost five years. We met through the Art Alliance."

"How often did you see each other?"

"Two or three times a week. But George insisted on returning home each night. He was a fanatic about appearances."

"Did you know he contacted me about arranging his disappearance?"

"I wasn't sure it was you, but I knew he had this harebrained idea."

"You didn't support him?"

"Absolutely not. I was urging him to come out of the closet. If he could only have been honest about his sexuality, none of that subterfuge would have been necessary. He wouldn't even consider coming out. Said he had his company to think of. I said that he owned more than half the stock; he didn't exactly have to worry about being fired. But George just couldn't do it. He'd started from scratch, you know. From poverty, or near poverty. He had a break with his parents and they never really forgave him. I think he never stopped trying to prove himself in their eyes, even after they died. For George, success was determined by how other people saw him, not by what he himself felt. If other people saw him as rich and powerful, then he *was* rich and powerful. But if they saw him as weak or vulnerable, then he was weak and vulnerable."

"But being gay doesn't mean being weak and vulnerable."

"I tried to explain that to him. But he felt that others would see it that way—as evidence that he was weak, that he was a failure." Arnot seemed overcome with sadness. Joe D. waited a few moments before asking, "Who else knew about you and Samson?"

"No one. I swear."

"Not even Mona Samson?"

"She knew about his sexual orientation. How could she fail to? It humiliated her. I think her worst fear was that George's homosexuality would come out into the open. She dreaded the idea of looking in the public's eye like some long-term beard." Arnot smiled, apparently relishing the thought. "I think she even encouraged the idea that George had girlfriends. In their set, everyone has lovers. It's only lovers of the same sex that embarrass."

"Is Samson really dead?"

Arnot took a deep, steadying breath. "Yes, I'm afraid so." He sounded convincing.

"But the five million dollars in the Cayman Island bank?"

"We've been through this. That money is earmarked for the Caribbean League."

"I can't find any record of them anywhere."

"Then dig a little deeper, why don't you," Arnot replied icily.

"The night Samson was murdered, did he mention meeting with me the day before?"

"He whispered something about the fact that he was still looking for a way out. That's what he called this crazy scheme of his. A way out."

"But he didn't indicate that he'd actually found a way out?"

Arnot shook his head.

"The cabdriver managed to write the letter *G* on his cab sheet before he was interrupted. Do you have any idea where George was going."

"I assume he was going home."

"Could he have been coming here?"

"*G* as in Gramercy, you mean?"

Joe D. nodded.

"If he were coming here we'd have shared a cab, wouldn't we?"

"Not if Samson had been afraid of being seen with you."

"Maybe things would have turned out differently if I had been there." Arnot's voice thickened here. "But George was on his way home that night. He always went home. Or he said he was."

Arnot stood up and left the room. Joe D. heard him blow his nose and sniffle a few times. He didn't know whether to be touched or suspicious.

Arnot returned and stood in front of Joe D., one hand resting on a chair. Once again Joe D. was surprised by the unexpected power of Arnot's body. If his face had an immature fleshiness to it, his body, sheathed in the thin silk robe, looked strong and sinewy. "These have been the hardest weeks of my life," he said, as if answering a question Joe D. had posed. "I haven't been able to grieve publicly, you see. No one knew about our relationship, so it would hardly do for me to break down sobbing in front of employees or friends, would it? It's almost as if George never existed at all. I remember at his funeral, how people swarmed around Mona, offering condolences. No one swarmed around me. Oh, one or two people came over and mentioned how tragic this was for the New York Art Alliance. But I couldn't exactly start to sob in front of them, could I? One doesn't sob at the loss of a benefactor, does one? *Benefactor.*" Arnot choked over the word. "He was that in more ways than one."

There was something undeniably theatrical about this

speech, but Joe D. didn't know whether Arnot was habitually theatrical or was putting on a show for his benefit. He did know that he wanted out of the apartment ASAP. But first he had one question.

"Do you recognize this person?" He took the photo of Arthur Rudolph, Senior, out of an envelope he'd brought along.

Arnot studied it for a moment before shaking his head. "Should I?"

"I guess not," Joe D. answered.

He walked back to the apartment, enjoying the morning air and the first tentative rays of what promised to be a warm sun. Arnot had depressed him, and as he walked he tried to figure out why. Was he responding to Arnot's grief at losing his lover? Or was he sensing the hollowness of his emotions, the insincerity? Arnot was hard to read. Like his apartment, which had been carefully decorated to look as if it hadn't been decorated so much as thrown together, Arnot seemed a bit too deliberately arranged, even when apparently distraught.

TWENTY-SEVEN

There was a note pinned by a magnetized bagel to the refrigerator when Joe D. got back. "I love you. Call about the phone message. Very intriguing. Alison."

Joe D. rewound the tape machine, wondering who would leave an intriguing message this early in the morning—it was still barely nine. The tape clicked into position and he heard Estelle Ferguson's voice. She sounded as if she were whispering.

"It's Estelle. Listen, there's something I want to show you. I'm already at my desk. It's seven-thirty. Something's about to happen, I'm sure of it. Tomorrow. Could we get together during lunch today? I could meet you at the same place we met last time. Call as soon as you get back." A long pause. "I hope I'm doing the right thing."

Joe D. dialed the Alliance's number and was connected to Estelle's extension. He heard a click on the line and knew the call was being forwarded to another desk. "Estelle Ferguson's line." The woman's voice sounded annoyed at having to cover for Estelle.

Joe D. asked for her and was told she wasn't in yet. He asked if she were sure about this, and she replied, testily, that she was positive. He hung up without leaving a message and tried Estelle's apartment. No answer.

Joe D. tried to hail a cab across town, but 9:00 was the tail end of rush hour and taxis were scarce. He ran to the cross-town bus stop, but was too impatient to wait, and started to jog towards Central Park. At Fifth Avenue there was still no sign of the bus so, reluctantly, he entered the park and jogged to the West Side. He arrived at the New York Art Alliance building out of breath. Fortunately, it was only mildly warm and he was only mildly damp.

He waved to the receptionist and kept on running up the broad staircase. He trotted down the hallway towards Arnot's office and stopped in front of Estelle's desk. It was empty. All the way over from the East Side Joe D. had been hoping against hope that she'd be there, that after calling him she'd stepped out for a bagel or something. The sight of the empty desk dashed these hopes.

The top of her desk was a jumble of papers and stray pens and paper clips. He didn't know about Estelle's work habits, but he knew that a lot of secretaries liked to tidy up their desks before leaving for any length of time. Estelle's desk looked as if she'd left it assuming she'd be back in a few minutes. Arnot's door was closed. Joe D. sat in Estelle's chair and began sorting through the papers on her desk. Most had to do with New York Art Alliance business—requests for grants, acknowledgments of grants, personnel matters. He opened the top drawer and discovered that Estelle was in fact a very neat person. Papers were perfectly stacked, pens lined up in a neat row, envelopes squarely sorted by size. He found nothing, however, that might have precipitated her anxious phone call.

He went through her drawers quickly, wondering whether Arnot was behind the closed door or simply hadn't come in yet. Perhaps he needed more time to recompose himself after their morning chat. He hadn't expected to find anything on the desk, but couldn't help feeling disappointed. Then he noticed a small slip of paper poking out from under several larger papers. He pulled it out and was surprised to find his initials—"J.D."—written over a phone number. Arnot's door opened at that moment, and Joe D. balled up the paper in his palm.

"What the hell are you doing here?"

Arnot looked pale and drawn. Even at the depth of his sobbing earlier he hadn't looked this bad.

"Where's your secretary, Arnot?"

"What business is that of yours?"

Joe D. stood up and slipped past Arnot into his office. He looked around. . . . for what? For Estelle Ferguson, bound and gagged on the sofa? Bleeding on the oriental carpet? Instead, he found the office as neat as it always was.

Arnot followed him into the office and closed the door behind him. "I demand an explanation," he said, but his voice was less authoritative than weary.

Joe D. decided to tell the truth. He sensed that Estelle was in trouble, and if she were in trouble then it was no secret—to somebody, at any rate—that she and Joe D. were in touch. "Estelle called me this morning," he said. "Early, around eight-thirty."

Arnot turned away, but Joe D. had caught the look of alarm on his face. He decided to scrap the truth temporarily. "I guess you know what she told me," he said with deliberate vagueness.

Arnot still had his back to Joe D. "I have no idea what she told you. If you think she was involved in anything illegal. . . ."

"You're the one embezzling funds from the Alliance." Joe D. wondered how long he could keep this going without having to reveal that he and Estelle had never actually spoken that morning.

Arnot spun around, a new glint of resolve in his eyes. "If Estelle told you something incriminating, then why aren't you here with the police, tell me that?"

"Where is she?" Joe D. asked.

"No one's seen her this morning."

"Does she ever leave her desk without telling you?"

"Only to make copies or get coffee."

"If I don't hear from her in an hour, I'm calling the police."

Arnot nodded solemnly a few times. "If you think you have to."

"It would be a lot easier if you'd tell me what happened to her."

"I don't know," he practically wailed. He either knew the truth, and was distressed by it, or was in the dark, and was distressed by that. In either case he looks as if he's about to collapse, Joe D. thought, as he left Arnot in his office. He stopped again at Estelle's desk to call in to his answering machine. Alison had called, still intrigued by the phone message she'd heard, but there were no new messages from Estelle Ferguson.

TWENTY-EIGHT

Joe D. questioned a few of the Alliance employees to find out if anyone had seen Estelle that morning. None had. The earliest to arrive had been a grants administrator with an office just off the main foyer on the first floor. She'd arrived at 8:15. The New York Art Alliance was not, apparently, a beehive of early risers.

Joe D. caught a bus back to the East Side. A cab would have been quicker but, despite a growing sense of alarm about Estelle Ferguson, Joe D. wasn't quite sure what to do. The bus ride gave him a chance to think.

He thought. Arnot wasn't responsible for Estelle's disappearance. She had called Joe D. at 8:30 and, one way or another, had left the Alliance building before the first employee arrived at 8:15. Since Joe D. had been with Arnot until about 7:45, it seemed very unlikely that he could have raced over to the Alliance headquarters and . . . and what? He chose not to follow this thought to its conclusion. He didn't want to think about what might have happened to Estelle, and all because she'd tried to contact him.

He absentmindedly massaged the pants pocket in which he'd shoved the balled up paper with his name and number on it. *All because she'd tried to contact him.* He retrieved the paper and smoothed it out, barely noticing it. Were these the last words she'd written before disappearing, his name and number? He refolded the paper and was about to put it back in his pocket when something struck him. He unfolded the scrap and looked at it. In his haste to dispose of the paper before Arnot saw it, Joe D. hadn't read it too closely. He'd noticed his initials, and assumed the number below them was his.

Bad assumption.

The initials were his, abbreviated. But the telephone number was not.

The bus lumbered through Central Park, and Joe D. wished to god he'd taken a cab. Fifth Avenue. Madison. Park. At Lexington he got off and ran the rest of the way along Sixty-sixth Street, easily outpacing the bus. Then he headed up Second and reached the apartment a few minutes later.

His answering machine greeted him dumbly, without a blink. He called the Alliance and was put through to Arnot, who answered his own phone: a bad sign. Sure enough, Estelle still hadn't shown up. He tried her apartment. Still no answer. Then he dialed the number Estelle had written on the slip of paper.

"Airways Charter." A woman's voice.

Joe D. had to stop and catch his breath. He used the interval to try to figure out why Estelle had written his initials above the telephone number of Airways Charter. She must have wanted him to call the company. Why?

"Airways Charter, hello?"

In an instant he devised a strategy. "Yeah, uh, this is Stuart Arnot." Joe D. held his breath.

"Yes, Mr. Arnot," the woman said casually, but with no recognition. "This is Karen Schmidt. How may I help you?"

"I just wanted to reconfirm the arrangements we had made."

He heard her type on a keyboard. "We have no arrangements made under the name Arnot, sir."

"Gee, my secretary must have made the arrangements under another passenger's name. Try Samson."

More typing. "No Samson."

The strategy was faltering. "This is a jet charter service, isn't it?" he said, stalling.

"That's right." She was beginning to sound annoyed.

"Maybe you could read me the names of the people who've reserved flights for today and tomorrow, and then I'll know what name my secretary booked us under. We're a large party."

He heard a big, tired sigh on the other end: 9:15, and already hassles. "Today we have jets for Anderson, Popejoy, and Finley. Tomorrow we have Berkeley, Roberts, Rudolph, Sonnenberg . . ."

A flash went off inside his head. He gripped the receiver tighter, as if it might fly out of his hand. "Arthur Rudolph?"

"Arthur Rudolph and one other passenger."

"Whose name is . . ."

"It doesn't indicate. Say, if you're on the flight, you should know that."

"I'm the other passenger," he said quickly.

"And I thought you said you were with a large party."

He couldn't think of anything to say to this, so he ignored it. "What time are we due to take off?"

"Eight A.M. from Butler Aviation in Queens. In a Cessna Eight-Ten. Arriving Grand Cayman at noon. There's a one-hour time difference. I hope you're not planning on changing your arrangements again. We've already had to reschedule two of our pilots to accommodate Mr. Rudolph once."

"No, no changes. I just want to make sure everything is

correct, that's all." Joe D. felt a kind of lightheadedness come over him. This made it difficult to scribble everything she'd just said.

"Well, is everything correct or isn't it?"

"What date were we originally scheduled for?"

"The day after tomorrow. But Mr. Rudolph called this morning to move it up a day."

"Mr. Rudolph called?"

"That's right."

"Did Mr. Rudolph leave a phone number, Karen?"

"Yes, he did." She read him the number, which he copied down.

"How is Mr. Rudolph planning on paying for the charter?"

"My records indicate in cash."

"How much is the flight?"

"I really don't know if I'm . . ."

"Mr. Rudolph's an employee, you see. He may be paying up front, but I'll be reimbursing him later."

"Well . . . it's eight thousand dollars, plus a fuel surcharge and landing fees."

"In cash, you say? Isn't that unusual?"

"Not at all," she said, then quickly added, "Well, *some* people pay in cash." Drug dealers, mostly, Joe D. guessed. No wonder she regretted sharing this information with him.

"What about immigration?"

"What about it?"

"Do you require a passport or anything?"

"We just deliver our passengers. Immigration and whatnot are their problem. Is there anything else?"

There better not be, her tone warned him. And in fact there wasn't.

Joe D. hung up and dialed the number she had given him. After two rings it picked up. The voice was uncharacteristically hoarse, and there was an urgent breathiness to it. But he recognized it at once, and he wasn't surprised. Joe D. hung up without identifying himself. The voice belonged to Stuart Arnot.

TWENTY-NINE

Joe D. called Arnot a few minutes later on his non-private line, this time to see if there was any news about Estelle. He considered asking him about his travel plans, but he was tired of hearing lies. It was like watching a rerun of a TV show you didn't particularly enjoy the first time around. Besides, another plan was taking shape in his head.

"It's Joe D. Heard from Estelle?"

"Not yet."

"You must be getting worried."

"Not really," Arnot said. Then, as if realizing how his indifference must sound, he added, "Well, of course, I'm *concerned.* But I'm sure Estelle had a doctor's appointment she forgot to tell me about."

Joe D. hung up and called a New York City cop he knew from his days on the Waterside force. A couple of years ago Charlie Dinofrio had been working on a drug case that involved a small-time runner who lived on the South Shore. Joe

D. had been assigned to help Dinofrio nail the guy, which basically involved sitting in a car for three days a half-block from his house and reporting any unexplained movements. There *was* an unexplained movement, as it turned out. Two guys in silk suits arrived one morning carrying briefcases. They didn't look like Avon ladies, so Joe D. radioed his captain, who called Dinofrio, who arrived, by helicopter, a half hour later. A bust was made, while Joe D. watched, under orders not to interfere, from half a block away. Dinofrio had told him that if he ever needed a favor . . .

"I need a favor."

"Shoot," Dinofrio said.

Joe D. wanted to get to the point, but felt he had to fill Dinofrio in on a few things. He quickly told him about his move to Manhattan, about opening a detective agency, and finally about working on the Samson murder.

"Cut and dried," Dinofrio interrupted. "A hijacking."

Joe D. wasn't about to argue with him. Nobody likes having their work second-guessed, cops included. "Probably. But in the meantime there's this secretary who's been helpful to me, Estelle Ferguson. She's turned up missing, and I wanted to report it to the cops without too many questions, know what I mean?"

Dinofrio did know, and he promised to look into it with a minimum of fuss.

His civic duty done, Joe D. planned his evening, beginning with a call to Alison. She chided him for not calling earlier to explain about Estelle's message, which she'd overheard while getting dressed that morning. She was suitably alarmed.

"I have to work tonight," he said, sounding like the corporate lawyer he always suspected she wanted him to be.

"None of this breaking and entering stuff, I hope," Alison said, hitting the nail on the head.

"I have to dictate a letter, take a meeting, then entertain clients over dinner at the Four Seasons. The usual."

"Very funny. Be careful."

* * *

He figured New York Art Alliance employees were not the late-working types—most probably had cocktail parties or openings scheduled. Joe D. decided he'd drop by at around 9:00. He'd worked a few things out, knew there were still some unresolved issues, and was convinced that the solution to the whole mess was in the New York Art Alliance building. He'd been brained there, Estelle Ferguson had disappeared from there, and in both instances one thing bothered him (other than the lump on the back of his head, which still made brushing his hair a trial): How did the person or persons responsible for these acts know that he'd be there when he was, and that Estelle had just called him when she did?

The answer, he knew, was in the building itself.

The afternoon loomed, long and empty, like most of his afternoons pre-Samson. Joe D. changed into shorts and a T-shirt and jogged over to the park. He'd already jogged through the park once today, racing over to the Alliance building, but he still felt charged with a restless energy that only further exercise would diffuse. He circled the reservoir twice and then, having killed only a half hour, trotted around it a third time. On his way back to the apartment, he walked down Fifth Avenue on the park side, and stood opposite Mona Samson's building for a few minutes. He counted windows up to her floor and stared dumbly at it for a while. Of all the people in this case he guessed that she alone knew the whole story. But she wasn't talking, not surprisingly. The row of windows along the eleventh floor appeared grimly impassive. The afternoon sun glanced off them, creating a hollowed-out look, as if the building was just a facade, with nothing but empty space behind it.

He got back to the apartment and showered. Enforced idleness is never easy to take. But it's purgatory when you know that things are happening that affect you, but over which you have no control. Joe D. could practically hear the players in the Samson case buzzing around him, plotting and conspiring. And he knew the window of opportunity for him to be effective was closing quickly. At 8:00 tomorrow morning a plane was taking off. Among its cargo was the solution to the Samson case.

Of course, even if tonight turned out to be worthless, he'd do his best to make sure the plane didn't take off. He figured he could call Dinofrio, who'd have contacts with the immigration people. But Joe D. suspected there would be no obvious reason for the authorities to delay the plane. A vision of the Cessna taking off over Queens haunted the periphery of Joe D.'s mind all afternoon.

He retrieved his gun from its home at the back of the bottom drawer of his dresser. It was a semiautomatic Beretta, his first purchase after leaving the Waterside force, and its dense weight never failed to reassure him, though he hoped to god he wouldn't have to use it. Alison regarded it as she would a pet boa constrictor, and had been urging him to store it in a safety deposit box. Still stalling for time, he gave it a good cleaning and then strapped it on, using a leather harness. He put a jeans jacket on over it and left for the West Side.

He arrived at the Alliance building at 8:00. He stood across the street from it and was gratified to find that all the lights were off. He used Estelle Ferguson's key to unlock the front door and punched in the alarm code. It was déjà vu all over again, a thought he found not at all comforting.

He was looking for something larger than bank statements tonight, but he suspected that Arnot's office was the place to begin this time too.

The silence that cloaked the dignified old building was as palpable as a jackhammer to Joe D.'s alert ears. This time, he *knew* he wasn't alone.

Arnot's office door was closed but unlocked. Joe opened it, walked in, and half expected to see Arnot behind his big desk. Arnot wasn't there, but Joe D. sensed a recent presence. It took a few moments for him to figure out why. There was a faint, barely perceptible aroma of woman's perfume. And something else almost but not quite masking it. An acrid smell, metallic. The combination of the two odors was very unpleasant and inexplicably alarming.

Joe D. stood in the center of the room and turned slowly. He stopped when he was facing a door at the end of the office farthest from Arnot's desk. In the three times he'd been in this office the door had never been open. He crossed the room and tried the door. It was locked. He left the office for the hallway opposite Estelle Ferguson's desk, and tried to gauge the size of the space that lay behind the door. The hallway in which Estelle's desk sat extended ten or eleven feet beyond Arnot's office, unless the building suddenly narrowed, which Joe D. doubted. That meant that the door led to a space considerably larger than a closet. If the hidden room was as wide as Arnot's office, it would be a bit too large for a private bathroom, but a good size for a private conference room. It was certainly worth taking a look at. Definitely worth it.

He returned to Arnot's office and studied the lock for a moment. It appeared to be the original lock, located just below the door handle. Not in the same league as a Medeco, he thought with relief, but he still regretted returning the skeleton keys and picks to Carmine. He took an explorative lunge at the door, which proved surprisingly resistant. His right shoulder, on the other hand, proved rather tender. He massaged it for a bit, psyching himself for a second attempt. This time he felt the door give a bit. His shoulder gave too, and was now throbbing. He made the third attempt with his left shoulder. This one really killed him, but at least he'd learned something that would doubtless prove invaluable down the road: Righties should never attempt to break down a door with their left shoulders. Someday he'd ask an orthopedist for an explanation.

Joe D. took a breather and walked back into the hall just to make sure his siege hadn't brought any visitors. Apparently not. He returned to the door and decided that the fourth attempt would be the last, but that he'd give it everything he had. He backed up an extra few steps, formed a mental image of that Cessna preparing to take off, and hurled himself at the door. Something snapped and, mercifully, it appeared not to be inside Joe D.'s body. A crack appeared along the seam of the door. Joe D. kicked violently at the keyhole, regretting that he'd worn sneakers that day. He kept on kicking until the chunk of wood that held the lock mechanism separated from the rest of the door. He took a breath, or tried to, and entered the sanctum sanctorum.

He knew immediately that he wasn't alone. He also sensed right away that whatever menace the room held had been dissipated. He sensed this even before he saw the bodies: The room felt dead but not deadly.

The first body he spotted was male. It was slumped over a long mahogany conference table. A pool of blood had formed around the torso and was dripping onto the beige wall-to-wall carpet. Joe D. put his hand on the body's back and felt a trace of warmth but no breathing; he hadn't been dead very long.

Joe D. had handled a corpse before, so he should have expected some difficulty as he tried to flip it over. But he was still surprised at its weight. It had the supple heaviness of a commercial-sized bag of fertilizer. Now he understood the term *dead weight.* Trying his best not to splatter blood on him, Joe D. grabbed the polo shirt the corpse was wearing and tried to flip it. He succeeded only in half undressing it. Reluctantly, he wedged his hands under the body and heaved it over. The head, unfortunately, lolled against the table a moment after the body, making a thud that was set off a sympathetic shudder in Joe D.

He knew right away who it was. Not from the back of the shadowy limousine, but from the obituaries. The corpse was George Samson. Given that two weeks was an awfully long time for a corpse to remain warm, it looked like Samson had succeeded in faking his death after all. Succeeded once, that is, and then failed.

There appeared to be a single bullet hole right about where Samson's heart was, but his chest was a mess, and there could well have been a second or even third hole nearby. There were some scratches and abrasions on Samson's right forearm. Joe D. guessed that Samson might have been holding a gun that someone had forcibly taken from him. Joe D. also noticed a big chunk of plaster blown out of the wall behind the table—further evidence of a struggle that had sent at least one bullet flying in a random direction. The metallic odor was more intense in this smaller, windowless room, and Joe D. decided it must be from the gun that was used to kill Samson. He looked around, but the gun, not surprisingly, was nowhere to be found. There was much else of note, however. The room was cluttered with clothing, empty food containers, magazines, newspapers, glasses, plates, utensils. Samson had obviously been living here for some time.

There was a phone at the opposite end of the room. Joe D. was about to use it to call the police when something caught his eye. Amid the mess in one corner of the room was a woman's pocketbook. He didn't recognize it, but he easily guessed whose it was. He picked it up and removed the wallet. It was Estelle Ferguson's.

Joe D. figured she couldn't be far from her pocketbook, and he was right. There was a small closet at the end of the room. He hesitated before opening it. Inside, slumped against the wall in a sitting position, knees crammed up to her face, was Estelle Ferguson. The grayness of her pallor told him that she was dead. So did the faint but nasty odor that drifted up from her. He saw no sign of a bullet, but there appeared to be cuts around her neck. She'd apparently been strangled with a rope or belt. The look on her face, mouth agape, eyes wide open and crossed in horror—he'd read somewhere that you could always tell if a person had suffered before dying from the expression on the corpse's face. Estelle had suffered. Joe

D. doubted whether he'd ever forget the look on her lifeless face. In fact, he forced himself to stare at her for a moment or two to make sure of it. He felt responsible for Estelle's murder, and knew that eventually he'd have to deal with this. Right now there were more urgent things to think about, but he wanted to be certain he'd remember what she'd been through. Her expression told him everything he needed to know.

He picked up the phone and started to dial when he heard someone enter Arnot's office. He replaced the receiver and took the Beretta out from its chest harness. He crossed the conference room and positioned himself behind the battered open door, the gun pointing upwards next to his head. He heard the person cross Arnot's office to the door. Then he saw the outline of someone through the gap between the door and the frame. The figure froze behind the door. Joe D. could hear it breathing. He held his own breath.

"Oh my god," he heard. Before he could place the voice, the figure ran to the body of George Samson and froze before it. Stuart Arnot stood over the corpse of his lover, open hands framing the sides of his head, his face nearly as agonized as that of Estelle Ferguson. "Oh my god, no. Oh god."

THIRTY

Joe D. stepped out from behind the door, replacing the gun in its shoulder holster. Arnot didn't seem to notice him. He continued to stare at the body of George Samson as if he expected it to return to life at any moment. Or perhaps he was trying to inure himself to the idea that Samson never would come to life. Joe D. figured these would be the last moments of privacy Arnot would have for a long, long time, so he didn't say anything for a few minutes. Instead he watched the man, and compared the grief he was witnessing now with the false grief he's seen earlier, in Arnot's apartment, when he'd pretended to be mourning his lover. Watching the real thing, it was hard to believe he'd been fooled earlier.

Finally, Joe D. broke the silence. "Why don't you tell me the whole story."

Arnot turned to look at him. He seemed not the least surprised to see Joe D. there; he was probably shockproof at this point.

"We came so close," he said in a half whisper.

"Tomorrow morning you were supposed to be on your way to the Caymans."

He looked at Joe D., surprised. "We never planned to harm anyone."

"A man was killed in the back of the cab. Not to mention the driver. You stole money from the New York Art Alliance. You caused pain to Samson's family. . . ." Even as Joe D. said this he heard the falseness in it. So did Arnot, who grasped at this one bit of hypocrisy to avoid dealing with the real suffering he'd caused.

"Pain to his family?" Arnot wiped a fist of tears from his face. "That's a laugh. His wife never cared about him. Neither did Joanna. No one cared about George except me. It was the tragedy of his life, really. He kept himself totally aloof from people because he had a secret side to him that he couldn't share."

"And the two people who were killed in the cab?"

"I had nothing to do with that," Arnot said, his voice turning earnest. A survivor's instinct was kicking in, pushing out grief. "He was supposed to disappear. When I heard about those two people . . ."

"At the board meeting that night, you had no idea what was going to happen?"

Arnot shook his head. "George knew I'd veto any plan that involved violence. He left at about nine that night and was back here a few hours later. He told me everything was taken care of, that he'd need to stay here until he could arrange for a plane. When I read in the paper about what happened, I was appalled. I asked George who the man was, the one that was killed in his place. He said it was some bum he'd dragged off the sidewalk. And that poor driver!"

"Why did Samson wait so long to leave the country?"

"We were going to leave last week. Then George found you nosing around in my office looking at bank receipts. He wanted to make sure everything was OK before leaving. If you had uncovered what we did, with the five million, George said he had an alternative plan."

"What was that?"

"I don't know exactly. I suppose Mona would have gotten us some more money somehow."

Joe D. didn't know whether or not to buy Arnot's innocent bystander role. He'd leave that to the police. "Mona had to identify the body, so she obviously knew George wasn't dead."

"She was in it all along. She wanted George out of the way as much as he wanted to *be* out of the way."

"And Estelle Ferguson?"

Arnot glanced over at the open closet, closed his eyes, and took a deep, unsteady breath. "I feel terrible about that. Do you have any idea what it was like working in this office all day, knowing that my secretary . . ."

Joe D. couldn't muster much sympathy for Arnot. "What happened to her?"

"She came in early today. George heard her searching my office, and then he heard her call you and leave a message. When she left her desk for the ladies' room he found a note on her desk with some information he'd written on it about the plane charter. I suppose George must have left it lying around. She must have found it yesterday evening and come in early today to see what else she could find. George strangled her with his belt. Poor Estelle!"

He sat down heavily and began to sob. It must be tough to discover that your lover is a cold-blooded murderer. It's bad enough to fake your own death. But to kill three people in the process puts you in a whole new league. Maybe Arnot was having second thoughts about his lover. Maybe he wasn't as innocent as he professed—at the very least he had defrauded the New York Art Alliance.

"When you got to the Caymans, you were planning to take the money you'd stolen and . . ."

"We never stole anything. That was George's money. We used the Alliance to, I don't know, *process* it. . . ."

"The technical term is *launder.*"

"You know what I mean. If George had simply sent the money to the Caymans, the IRS might have questioned it. By donating it to the Art Alliance he made sure that no one noticed."

"There was an added bonus: Samson got a tax deduction." Joe D. had to smile, but Arnot didn't see the humor. He looked as if he were about to defend his late lover, then thought better of it.

"You know, one thing's been bothering me. Five million dollars doesn't seem like a lot of money to live on for the rest of your lives. Not compared to what Samson was used to."

Arnot nodded. "Money was never George's thing, except that he knew it was the yardstick by which others measured him. Mona was the one who liked money, and what it bought. George and I could have lived very comfortably on the interest from five million. . . ." He broke off here, his voice faltering. "There were some liquid assets too," he added, regaining his composure. "Some jewelry, a few rare coins. They're at my apartment. I was to bring them along tomorrow." Arnot glanced almost wistfully at Samson's body, and then back at Joe D. "Did you kill him?"

"He was dead when I got here. Newly dead. Any idea who could have done it?"

Arnot looked almost lovingly at the body and shook his head, as if wondering who would want to harm such an angel.

"Who else knew he was living here?"

Arnot shrugged. Then his face turned suddenly nasty. "Mona," he spat. "Other than me, she's the only one."

"But why would she bother killing him when he was already dead?" The absurdity of this statement was lost on neither of them.

"You'll have to ask her that."

"Why did you come here tonight?"

"Visiting. I made a point of leaving the office at the usual time, to avoid suspicion. Then I'd return with some food and George and I would spend a few hours . . ."

He fell into a funk, and Joe D. left him to wallow there while he called Dinofrio at his home number. Donofrio said he'd call the appropriate precinct. Joe D. left Arnot with the corpses and headed for the front door. He didn't think Arnot would run—where could he go, now?—and he didn't want to be around when the cops arrived, though he knew he'd have to answer questions eventually.

On the sidewalk he flagged a cab, and gave the driver Mona Samson's address.

THIRTY-ONE

Joe D. didn't recognize the doorman on duty that night. He paced the building's outer vestibule while he was announced upstairs. It was past 11:00 when he was finally admitted to the Samson apartment by Mona herself. She was wearing a floor-length cream-colored satin robe. Her hair was pulled back tightly into a small knot behind her head, making her look as fierce and alarmed as a raccoon caught in headlights.

"I assume you have a good reason for disturbing me at this hour?"

Joe D. told her he hoped so. She stood in the large entrance gallery with her arms crossed against her fleshless chest. The marble shimmered like melting ice. The chandelier overhead was turned to a very dim setting, and what little light it gave off was absorbed by the lustrous, blue-black lacquered walls. Against this backdrop, in her flowing robe, the stationary Mona Samson resembled a Greek statue. A very narrow statue. She seemed disinclined to let him any further into the apartment. Joe D. wondered if she were alone.

"Your husband's been murdered," Joe D. began.

"Tell me something I don't know," she said in her cool, ageographical accent.

"He was killed tonight. As I think you already know."

He saw a tremble form around her eyes. "You must be out of your mind."

"You knew your husband was alive—until tonight—because you identified the body. It wasn't his. I know that because I saw his body tonight. At the New York Art Alliance building, where he's been living since last week."

She said nothing at first, undoubtedly gauging what the proper response should be. Finally she spoke, in a faltering voice that betrayed an atavistic lilt. "The body I identified was my husband's."

"I'm telling you it wasn't."

"I think I'd recognize the man I've been married to for twenty-five years."

"From what I hear, you weren't exactly on intimate terms."

"Intimate enough to identify his corpse, I should guess." The affectless voice had returned. "Although I must say he was pretty beat up."

"We'll see about that. You'll probably have some more identifying to do in the morning. Too bad your husband's relatives wouldn't let you cremate him."

She glanced at the floor. Joe D. noticed ripples in the cream satin; she was breathing hard.

"Where were you earlier this evening?"

"Here."

"All night?"

"And most of the afternoon as well."

"You may have to prove this to the police."

"I have proof."

"In what form."

"Servants."

"You could slip out of this place with the silverware and no one would notice."

"I was with someone else, then."

"Who?" Although he already knew the answer.

"Mr. Williams was here all evening, if you must know. He's here now, in fact. Do you need to talk to him?"

What Joe D. needed to do was figure out who had killed Samson if Mona was in fact at home all evening. "Sure," he answered, figuring he had nothing to lose.

Mona left him through one of several doors leading off the gallery. A few minutes later she reappeared with Kendall Williams. He had on a tartan bathrobe that looked a few inches too short on him. Joe D. wondered if it had belonged to Samson. His hair was perfectly groomed, but his expression betrayed some anxiety.

"You wanted to see me," he said.

"I need to know where you and Mona were all evening."

"Together, in this apartment."

"As I explained to him," Mona chimed in.

Joe D. looked at them, standing next to each other in their robes. He wondered if Mona realized that she aged five or ten years with her lover by her side. She probably figured Williams had the opposite effect on her appearance. Or was it the reverse: Williams looked younger in her company? They were an unappealing couple in any case, like two inoffensive pieces of furniture that clashed when combined.

As alibis for each other they were perfectly complementary, however. And Joe D. believed them. The look in Mona's eyes when he told her what happened earlier that night was genuine. It wasn't alarm or sadness or even panic; instead it was a look of confusion, the look of a woman trying to catch up with events while deciphering what effect these events would have on her. It was easy to figure why both would be pleased with Samson's first "death." It was less easy to figure why they would scuttle the original plan by murdering Samson, especially when an actual murder would inevitably implicate Mona in the original scam.

"You realize that when you identify your husband's body tomorrow you'll be arrested for fraud."

"You're assuming I *will* identify my husband tomorrow."

"You could deny that it's George. But I doubt it would do you much good, other than stalling for time. Stuart Arnot will ID him. So will Joanna Freeling and a dozen other people who knew him."

"His body was so destroyed, and his face was covered with blood. . . ."

"Shut up, Mona," Williams interrupted. "You don't have to talk to him."

Mona looked at Williams, as if she were startled but pleased by his take-charge attitude. There was something else in that brief look: Gratitude at being able to place her fate into the hands of someone else, gratitude so profound it probably felt like love. "That's right," she said after a pause. "I don't need to speak to you. You can leave now, Mr. DiGregorio. Right now."

Two decades of assimilation evaporated from her voice, and traces of Mississippi came through like raw wood behind layers of peeling paint. Banishing him from her presence was perhaps the last imperious gesture she'd be allowed for some time, and Joe D. thought she knew it.

Alison was sleeping when he got home. Joe D. was tempted to wake her, but thought better of it. He wanted to talk things over with her, sort things out. She had a clear, logical mind, and her distance from the case would be valuable. But she had worked late tonight, and had to be up early tomorrow to open the store. He watched her sleeping, and resisted the urge to crawl into bed next to her. She was always so warm when she slept, a dense, reassuring warmth that would go a long way towards soothing his overworked mind. After a while he left the bedroom and got a beer from the refrigerator. He sat down at the dining room table with a pad and pen. He wrote the names of everyone involved in the Samson case, scattering them around the paper: Samson himself, Stuart Arnot, Mona Samson, Joanna Freeling, the Rudolphs—father and son—and Kendall Williams. Then he drew lines between them to show relationships. Each was connected to George Samson by a motive for killing him—either faking his murder or the actual deed. Several were connected to each other by lines of hate or jealousy or revenge or love. When he finished the paper, there was a tangle of lines with Samson at the intersection of all of them.

Joe D. thought he could figure out how the original "murder" of Samson went down. Mona was involved in that, if only by agreeing to misidentify the corpse. Arnot professed his innocence of the actual murders, and Joe D. believed him, though he'd be implicated for going along with the deception. But neither Mona nor Arnot had a motive for actually murdering Samson earlier this evening. What difference did it make to Mona, after all, if George was or wasn't dead, as long as everyone, including his executors, believed he was? And Arnot was about to join his lover in paradise with five million dollars. He wasn't even mentioned in Samson's will.

So who, then, had really killed Samson? Unless Joe D. had overlooked an obvious candidate, it came down to three people: Joanna Freeling or one of the Rudolphs. He circled their names on his pad and kept circling them until they stood out from the tangle of lines. He got himself a second beer and stared at the mess on the paper for a few more minutes.

Then he knew.

THIRTY-TWO

Room 12 in the New York City morgue had a surprisingly pleasant view of Lower Manhattan. Joe D. knew this because he found it easier to stare at the view than at the soon-to-be-opened coffin in the center of the room.

He didn't have to be there. When Dinofrio had set this up, he'd told Joe D. that he'd see that the proper people were in attendance. But Joe D. felt that he should be there. Not that he was in any doubt about the outcome. No, he wasn't feeling any suspense. Only dread at the prospect of the opened coffin.

A medical examiner was in the room along with an assistant. Both were women, both probably in their thirties, Joe D. thought, both sufficiently attractive and "normal" that Joe D. wondered several times that afternoon what they could possibly be doing in this line of work. He looked for a trace of ghoulishness in their faces, and found only professionalism mixed with some curiosity. Exhumations, after all, were a rarity.

In one corner was a Detective Rice, the cop who'd handled the original Samson murder. He looked distinctly uncomfortable, and Joe D. guessed it wasn't only the prospect of seeing a two-week-old body that was causing him to repeatedly hoist his pants up by the belt that hung loosely just below his voluminous gut. By late last night the 20th Precinct had had to admit that they'd erred on the Samson "murder." The body in the Art Alliance building was almost certainly Samson's—they had Stuart Arnot's word on this, and additional identifications would follow. The body buried under Samson's marker in a cemetery in Westchester had been hastily exhumed this morning, following a lengthy Q-and-A session involving Joe D., Mona Samson, Arnot, and a few lesser characters.

The coffin, a mahogany affair with brass handles, sufficiently expensive looking to hold the last remains of what had been thought to be a very rich and powerful man, looked none the worse for wear for its two weeks in Westchester's rocky soil. Someone must have cleaned it up before delivery, Joe D. thought. A little Pledge, a little elbow grease, and it was as good as new. If only the same were true of its contents.

The ME's assistant handed out white masks, which she said were to cover both mouths and noses. Joe D. gratefully put his on. "This may be a bit unpleasant," the ME said, but her voice revealed no trepidation.

She undid a pair of latches and opened the hood which, disappointingly, didn't creak a bit. The two physicians leaned over the coffin eagerly. Joe D. and Detective Rice both took an instinctive step backwards.

"Signs of midterm decomposition," the ME said. Her assistant reached for a pad and wrote this down, and began scribbling as the ME continued to discourse on the ravages that just two weeks' time had taken on the corpse.

"Doctor, if you don't mind, we're interested in the identity of the deceased, not his condition." Rice tried to speak with authority, but this was difficult, given that he couldn't bring himself to even look in the coffin's direction. Joe D. detected the first hint of an odor, a stale, earthy smell overlaid with something harsher, sharper, and made an effort to breathe through his mouth.

"We have to record this information," she snapped. "City regulations."

Mercifully, they were through in just a few minutes. This wasn't an autopsy, after all. The ME turned to Rice and Joe D., and asked if they wanted to take a look. He saw Rice's eyes widen in disgust before he steeled himself with a shrug and yet another hoist of his trousers. Both men sidled across the room toward the coffin and peeked around the opened lid. Rice looked for only a moment. "That's the guy was shot in the cab," he said, backing off.

Joe D. forced himself to look a bit longer. The corpse's flesh seemed to be shrinking around its skull, lending a sharpness to the features, a clarity, even. The skin was the color of an old bruise, with darker patches. Joe D. found himself pointlessly concentrating on the body's tie, a rich red-and-blue paisley—an easier focus than the corpse itself.

Could anyone have genuinely mistaken this figure for George Samson? Could Mona Samson? He'd never gotten a good look at Samson when he was alive, but in death there was a certain similarity. Both were large men with features that seemed out of proportion to their faces: Large though well-formed noses, big almond eyes, full lips. Still, Joe D. recognized the face. Mona must have also.

He turned to Rice. "Ask Mrs. Samson to come in."

A moment later she entered the room. She was wearing a maroon suit that was cinched around what there was of her waist, accentuating her thinness. She was perched atop the tallest pair of high-heeled pumps Joe D. had ever seen; a fall from these shoes could be fatal. She brought a bony hand to her face as soon as she entered. Joe D. grabbed a spare mask from a table and gave it to her. She stared at it a bit, as if wondering whether it complemented her outfit, before putting it on. Detective Rice led her over to the coffin, which she peered into with widened eyes, as if examining a ring in a Cartier's counter. Then she looked up at Joe D. and shook her head.

"Two weeks ago you thought that was your husband," Joe D. said. He could feel his breath rebounding off the mask, warming his face.

"He's been cleaned up since then. When I saw him he was a mess."

"Do you recognize this person?" Detective Rice asked.

She had backed away from the coffin a few steps. "No."

"You might want to take a second look, Mrs. Samson," Joe D. said.

"I have never seen this man before in my life," she said slowly.

"I think you have. And I think we'll be able to prove it."

Her lower face was covered, but her eyes expressed everything she felt about him, none of which was charitable.

"Bring in Rudolph now," Joe D. said. He watched Mona's reaction. Arthur Rudolph, Junior, had been kept in a separate room from her. Her eyes widened as she looked down at the floor. Now, surely, she knew what was coming.

Rudolph walked in looking haggard and scruffy. Joe D. handed him a mask, which he quickly put on. He glanced at Mona Samson but didn't appear to recognize her. Then, unbidden, he walked to the coffin and looked in.

He didn't appear to react at first. He stared as if looking at a great work of art or a rare fossil, fascinated but not moved.

"Your father?" Joe D. asked quietly.

Rudolph nodded, but showed no inclination to leave his father's side. Joe D. considered leaving them alone for a few minutes, but Rudolph Senior wasn't a pretty sight, and it would do Junior no good to spend more time than necessary with him. Joe D. took Rudolph by the elbow and led him past Mona and out of the room. He didn't resist. In fact, he almost glided along with Joe D. as if his willpower had vanished on seeing his father's putrefying body.

Rice joined them a moment later in the corridor. "We're going to have some questions for you. We'll find you an office to wait in while we deal with Mrs. Samson." Rudolph nodded blankly. Only when Mona joined them in the hallway and removed her mask did he react. Joe D. saw his whole body tense up. His face looked disgusted and ferocious at the same time. "Murderer," he hissed at her. He seemed about to move towards her. Rice placed a restraining hand on his arm. It didn't seem to take much force to keep him in place.

For her part, Mona averted her eyes and winced, as if she'd been confronted by a panhandler in front of her Fifth Avenue building. Joe D. decided he was looking forward to interrogating her with Detective Rice. Getting a reaction out of Mona Samson was a challenge he relished.

"This way, Mrs. Samson," Rice said. "We have some questions we'd like to ask."

THIRTY-THREE

They found a small, windowless conference room near the examination room. Mona immediately crossed the room and stood in a far corner. She looked small and trapped, but her face crinkled in distaste when Detective Rice asked her to take a chair, as if the mere sound of his voice offended her.

"I'll stand," she said.

"Suit yourself," Rice said, and took a chair. Joe D. remained standing.

Rice pulled his chair as close to the Formica table as his copious gut would allow, the chair legs scraping along the floor. He pressed the *record* button on a large tape recorder and then clasped his hands and looked up at Mona. He recited her Miranda rights while she gazed down at him with a combination of scorn and curiosity, as if he were a talking dog. When he was done, she clapped her hands slowly and almost noiselessly. "Well done, Detective. Well done."

Joe D. thought he saw Rice grin humbly. "Why don't you tell us what happened on the night of April twelfth?"

Mona seemed to recoil from the bluntness of the question. "The night my husband was murdered?" She saw Joe D. give her a look, and corrected herself. "The night I *thought* he'd been murdered. I've been through this with the police already last week."

She was remarkably collected for a woman who'd just seen a decomposing corpse only hours after identifying the body of her husband, not to mention the fact that she was up to her neck in a murder conspiracy. Joe D. decided Rice was no match for her, and hoped he was. "Mrs. Samson," Joe D. began, "you're in a lot of trouble."

A slight but unmistakably arrogant lift of her chin indicated that she would need more detail before she admitted to being in any kind of trouble.

"At the very least you misidentified the body of Arthur Rudolph last week. I don't care how beat up he was, you knew Rudolph and you knew it was his body. If you misidentified the body, you had to be in on your husband's disappearance scam. That scam involved two murders, Rudolph's and the cabdriver's. Even if you didn't pull the trigger . . ."

"I didn't," she inserted rashly.

Joe D. knew, then, that he had her. "Who did, then?"

Another arrogant lift of the chin.

"Look, you're as good as convicted for aiding and abetting. You might as well tell us what you know."

She stood there for a moment, staring over their heads at some point on the cream-colored wall near the ceiling. Joe D. could see her swaying slightly. She looked pathetic all of a sudden, and he knew she was going to talk.

"I want a lawyer," she said with a note of defiance.

Rice shoved a phone across the conference table in her direction. She took a small leather address book out of her pocketbook and dialed a number. She asked for Leonard Brody and was connected to him instantly; Joe D. guessed her calls were always taken promptly. He heard her tell her attorney where she was and watched her close her eyes impatiently as he doubtless responded to this news. A moment later she hung up and said he'd be there in fifteen minutes.

"Why don't you sit down and wait," Joe D. said. She looked so fragile, he was half afraid she'd keel over.

"We didn't want anyone to die," she said, as if in response. "When George contacted you two weeks ago, he was serious, you know. He had some scheme involving a car crash. He needed your help, though. Or someone's. I never knew the details. If you'd gone along, maybe none of this would have happened."

"There's no way I'm going to feel responsible for what you and your husband did," Joe D. said angrily.

"Of course not," she said almost sweetly. She was talking as if in a trance, her voice steady but unmodulated. "George was so desperate. He had to get out of his life, you see. He couldn't stand it any more."

"Maybe you want to wait for your lawyer to get here," Joe D. suggested.

She shrugged. "It's too late for that. I guess I knew this was bound to happen. Did you know that George and Stuart Arnot were lovers?"

She asked this almost matter-of-factly, as if reporting a bit of stale gossip. Joe D. nodded and wished she would express some genuine emotion. He'd know how to respond to that. Rice, in the meantime, was staring at her openmouthed.

"He was so frantic to get out of our marriage, sometimes I thought he might kill me." She chuckled silently, her face contorting into a wrinkle-free geography of bumps and bulges. "When he presented me with this scheme, the one involving Arthur Rudolph, I couldn't resist. It seemed to solve all our problems."

She paused, as if relishing the thought.

"The day of the New York Art Alliance board meeting I drove up to Westchester to get Arthur Rudolph out of that nursing home. George had hit on the brilliant idea of using Rudolph to replace him. They looked enough alike, and I, the widow, would be identifying the body. I was nervous about how Rudolph would react to seeing me. But we'd been told by the nursing staff that he was disoriented most of the time. George paid the bills for Rudolph, did you know that? I found Rudolph on the front lawn, just sitting there, half comatose if you ask me. He recognized me, though, the wife of his archenemy. I gave him this story about how Samson Stores was looking for a new CEO to replace George, about how the board wanted to interview him for the job. The poor man ate it up. It was his dream come true, the chance to get back in control. It was simple after that to get him into my car. I even convinced him to go back to his room to get his passport and wallet, which George had said he'd need."

"Where'd you take him after that?"

"I stored him at our country place for the rest of the day. At seven I drove him back into town. I parked in a lot on the West Side, and then we got into a cab, as planned, at exactly nine. I told him I'd drop him off wherever he wanted. He said he'd stay with his son."

"On Gansevoort Street," Joe D. interjected. "That's what the cabbie started to write down. *G* as in Gansevoort."

Mona shrugged at this now unimportant detail. "We picked George up outside the Art Alliance. A block later I got out."

"Rudolph couldn't have been too happy seeing your husband get into the cab with you."

"He was almost completely out of it. I'd given him a few drinks in the country, and he kept nodding off as we drove. He was heavily medicated to begin with. I think he was so confused by the time he saw George that he didn't know what was happening. In any case, I got out just a block after George got in."

"Didn't want to soil your clothes?"

"I never knew the driver would be shot. And Rudolph's better off dead anyway."

Still no sign of emotion. She might have been describing a boring dinner party to a friend. "But the driver could have identified you. You must have known he'd have to be killed."

"It was George's plan," she shot back.

Somehow Joe D. couldn't picture her as a passive participant. "Who else was in on this?"

"Stuart Arnot knew all about it, of course." She said his name as if it hurt her lips to pronounce it.

"And Williams?"

"No, he knew nothing." A surge of feeling seemed to overtake her momentarily. A second later it was gone. "He's innocent, I assure you."

"Did you know that your husband and Arnot were planning to leave the country tomorrow?"

She nodded. "They were planning to stop in Grand Cayman to make financial arrangements, and then they were going to some island nearby. George never told me which one. At that point he'd be as good as dead. Stuart was to stay only a week or two. When he got back he was going to resign from the Alliance and slowly end his life up here. Eventually he was to move to the Caribbean full time."

"And you'd be free to marry Williams."

"Oh, please. Anything but marriage." But she sounded nervous and insincere saying this, as if afraid to admit that marriage was what she really wanted.

"Then why did you go along with this, if you didn't want to remarry?"

She waited before answering. "Do you have any idea what it's like to live with someone, even in separate bedrooms, who finds you physically undesirable?" She paused, as if waiting for a response. "Physically *repulsive?*" Her voice quivered over the word, and she put a reedy arm on the table for support. "I couldn't take it anymore. I felt as if I were being reproached every day of my life. To half of New York I was the quintessence of style. To my husband I was a piece of baggage to have on his arm at social functions. But with Ken . . . with Kendall I felt like a woman. I felt desirable." Her voice dropped to a gruff whisper. "Loved."

As she spoke the polish in her voice peeled away to reveal deeper and deeper shades of Mississippi.

"I didn't even love George, really. Or maybe I did, who knows? I know he didn't love me. I could live with that. What I couldn't live with was knowing that he found me loathsome. When he proposed his scheme to me I had no choice. I couldn't go on living with him. One of us had to disappear."

"You must have known when you married him that . . ."

"Oh, I knew, I knew," she broke in. "I knew he had the money I needed to go where I wanted to go. When I met George he lived in three rooms in a high-rise on Third Avenue." She shook her head, as if she'd found him in a ghetto. "With white walls and these framed posters all over the place. And he had millions! I may have been only an assistant at an ad agency, but I knew it was a sin to waste the kind of money George had. And I knew how to spend it, put it to its best use." She smiled, and her eyes narrowed, as she recalled the pleasure of deploying her husband's assets. "As for the sexual part, I knew after a few dates that he wasn't interested in me that way. In any woman. I guess I figured I could, I don't know, *persuade* him. As it turned out, I could as easily have persuaded him to take a ninety-percent markdown on his entire inventory as make love to me." She chuckled bitterly at this. "Or maybe I thought I could live without that. . . . that part of marriage. So, when no one was looking we went our separate ways. And when they were looking, George held my hand and smiled and pretended he wouldn't rather be holding a dead cod."

Her voice was all drawl now, less Southern than merely tired, spent. She seemed to be relishing the chance to explain herself, and Joe D. worried that she had much more to explain. He didn't know how much more he could take, but he did have one more question.

"Still, Mrs. Samson, you drove up to Westchester and kidnapped Arthur Rudolph. . . . then you delivered him to his murderer. . . . all because your husband found you . . ." He hesitated before the word *repulsive,* and sought in vain for a gentler euphemism. "All because he was homosexual?"

"I suppose I could bear it so long as I saw no alternative. But once I'd met Ken . . . You know, dieters know that it's sometimes easier to lose weight by fasting than by eating just a little. Abstinence is easier to bear than resisting temptation. Before I met Ken I was fasting. Then I got a taste of what I'd been missing and I became desperate. I'd have done anything to get out of my marriage."

The door opened and a stocky, silver-haired man entered. Joe D. assumed it was Mona's attorney. He looked confused until he spotted his client in the corner. Then he looked startled. "My god, Mona, what's going on here?"

She looked broken, leaning against the table, her head bowed. She glanced up at her lawyer without betraying any relief at seeing him. "It's over. All over." *Ova, owl ova,* is how it came out. The dreamy quality of her voice made Joe D. think that she was referring not to the events of the past two weeks, but to her entire masquerade of a life. The houses. The clothes. The jewelry. The sham marriage.

Ova, owl ova.

THIRTY-FOUR

Joe D. and Detective Rice left Mona Samson and her lawyer, who had requested a private conference with his client. They headed for a nearby office where Rudolph, Junior, was waiting. Joe D. excused himself and looked for a pay phone. He dialed directory assistance and got the number for Airways Charter. Karen Schmidt answered, as she had before, and after just a few questions, she confirmed a theory Joe D. had been developing for the past twelve hours.

He hung up and went in search of Rudolph and Rice. He found instead a commotion in progress. Three or four cops were milling around an open doorway while others were fanning out along the corridors.

"What's happening?" Joe D. asked one of the cops.

"Guy bolted. A suspect or something."

Joe D. looked into the room. Rice was talking to two other cops in a small room that looked like it had recently been someone's office, but was now unoccupied. There was an oversized steel-case desk pushed against a wall covered with smudges where papers had once been taped up. Two guest chairs in flaking green vinyl were the only other pieces of furniture. "There you are," Rice said when he spotted Joe D. "Rudolph's gone."

"Shit," was all Joe D. managed.

"We'd'a had him under tighter security if we'd'a known he was a suspect," Rice said. "I thought we was just questioning him. *Was* he a suspect?"

"Still is," Joe D. said. "You searching the building?"

"My guys are. But we figure he's outta here by now. You got his home address?"

Joe D. gave it to Rice, but he didn't think Rudolph was headed home. He excused himself and walked quickly out of the building. He flagged a cab and gave the driver Joanna Freeling's address.

Joanna had never struck him as the forgiving type, so he wasn't surprised to find Rudolph in the vestibule of her building in Soho, whining into the intercom. He didn't seem to notice when Joe D. opened the outside door and joined him in the tiny space.

"Joanna, please. Just let me up. Please." His voice was faltering over every word. "Joanna, are you there?" He pressed the buzzer and held it for a few seconds. "Joanna, *please."*

A moment later the voice of Rudolph's Rapunzel crackled through the small metallic speaker. "Get the fuck out of my life," it said. Rudolph, far from being put off by this, seemed encouraged by her response. At least it showed she was listening. "Just five minutes, that's all. Five minutes and I'll go." But Joe D. had heard the intercom click off; she wasn't listening any more.

"Give it up, Arthur," Joe D. said calmly. Rudolph turned around slowly and looked at him, not a shred of surprise or anxiety evident. "I need to explain to her," he said pitifully.

"She doesn't want to hear."

"I've left notes for her, messages. Why won't she listen?"

Rudolph seemed to have an almost childlike belief in second chances; he seemed incredulous that Joanna wouldn't speak to him. And he seemed utterly convinced that five minutes with her would change her mind. Joe D. thought of her "paintings" and knew that Joanna Freeling was not a woman of vacillating convictions.

"You shouldn't have run out on the cops," Joe D. said evenly.

"But I had to see her."

"You're going to be arrested for George Samson's murder, you know that."

Rudolph nodded sadly. "How did you know?"

Joe D. was beginning to feel claustrophobic in the tiny, airless vestibule. And he couldn't be sure that Joanna wasn't listening in, not that it would make much difference. "How about I buy you a drink?"

Joe D. didn't wait for an answer. He took Rudolph by the elbow and led him back onto Grand Street. He remembered seeing a bar on Spring Street. They walked there together in silence. Inside, he put Rudolph at a table and ordered draft beer for both of them from the bartender. The bar was new but had been carefully decorated to look like a dive from the early fifties. It was just noon and the place was empty, which enhanced the seedy atmosphere the owners so coveted.

Joe D. drained half his beer while Rudolph simply regarded his, as if it offered a clue to something he needed to know. "Mona Samson had an alibi for last night," Joe D. began. "She was with her lover. Not the best alibi, I'll grant you, but then she had no reason for killing a man who was already supposed to be dead. I was with Samson's body when Arnot arrived. He'd have to be some actor to fake his reaction to seeing his lover's corpse. The only other people with a motive for making sure Samson was really dead were you and your father. I had a hunch your father was already dead. That left you."

"Process of elimination?" Rudolph said, almost fliply. "That'll really impress the DA." Joe D. was pleased that Rudolph was regaining some measure of self-defense. It was easier to take than moroseness.

"But I still had one question. How did you know that Samson was alive, and how did you know where to find him? Then it hit me. Samson was using your father's passport to leave the country. He booked the plane using your father's name. *Your* name, Arthur. So what I figure happened is this: Someone, either at the charter company or maybe Arnot's secretary, Estelle Ferguson, tried to contact Arthur Rudolph *Senior* and got you instead. And that led you to the New York Art Alliance yesterday evening."

Rudolph was nodding now, as if only dimly recalling the events Joe D. was describing.

"A while ago I called Airways Charter. Sure enough, the dispatcher had tried to contact Arthur Rudolph yesterday afternoon to confirm the flight that was supposed to take off this morning. Only the number she rang didn't answer. It was the number Stuart Arnot had given her, the private number in his office. No one but Stuart answered that line. If he isn't in his office, no one picks up. He must have been out of his office yesterday afternoon, when the dispatcher called. So she did the logical thing. She tried to call him at home. But "Arthur Rudolph"—Joe D. made quotes in the air—"hadn't left his home number. So she looked it up in the phone book. And called you. She got Junior instead of Senior, but she probably wasn't aware of this."

Joe D. waited for Rudolph to respond, but he didn't.

"That must have blown your mind, to find out that your father was chartering a plane to the Caymans. The dispatcher said she left a message on your answering machine, and that when you called her back it was almost six. Somehow you convinced her to give you 'your father's' office number—Arnot's private line. You called that number, didn't you? And who should answer but George Samson?"

"You have no proof of any of this," Rudolph said. But he sounded defeated.

"My guess is that Samson answered the private line after business hours." And why not? Estelle had told him it had only been installed a few weeks ago, more than likely in anticipation of Samson's hiding out in the office. Arnot was probably the only person who knew the number, though he must have given it to the charter company. "Did you recognize Samson's voice right away? Or did you just realize it wasn't your father?"

Rudolph said nothing.

"Look, you might as well answer. We have proof that you're one of only three people who knew where Samson was hiding out last night. The other two have alibis. You're screwed any way you look at things."

Rudolph considered this for a while. "I knew his voice the moment I heard it. It wasn't a conscious thing. Joanna and I had dinner with him a few times. When he answered the phone he said something like 'Is that you?' I guess he was expecting someone. I said something like 'George Samson, back from the grave.' There was a long silence. Then he hung up. I called right back. It rang forever before he answered. He didn't say anything, just picked up the receiver and listened. So I told him who I was, and that I knew who he was, and I was going to call the police. That's when he finally spoke. He told me he had my father with him, and that he'd kill him if I called the cops. He told me to come over and he gave me the address."

"You brought a gun with you?"

"No! I wasn't planning on killing him. I just wanted to find my father. Samson opened the door for me and took me upstairs to that office he was living in. I asked him where my father was. And he told me. He told me everything. How Mona had taken my father from his nursing home. How he'd murdered him in that cab. I couldn't believe what I was hearing. I guess I was too stunned to think what he was going to do next. What he did was pull a gun on me."

Self-defense, Joe D. thought, relieved. Rudolph had killed in self-defense. "He couldn't let you live, not when you knew he was still alive."

"As soon as I saw the gun I went crazy. I wasn't even scared, just crazy. Joanna, my father, now this. I went nuts. We were only a few feet apart and I just ran at him. He got one bullet off, but it missed me. I knocked the gun out of his hand and grabbed it. Then I shot him."

Rudolph's account of what happened jibed with the physical evidence—the scratches and abrasions on Samson's wrist, which he'd gotten trying to hold onto his gun, and the bullet hole in the plaster on one wall of the conference room. "Sounds convincing," he offered.

"It's the truth! I don't regret that I killed him, not after what he did to my father. He ruined his mind and then he killed him. I'd shoot him again if I could."

"I'd keep that thought to yourself." Rudolph was sweating now, as if, in recounting the events of yesterday, he was reliving them. "What did you do after you shot him?"

"I left the building and went back to my apartment. The gun's there, by the way. I didn't know what to do with it, so I took it with me."

"The police will want to look at it. If it was Samson's, it's bound to be the same gun used to kill your father and the cabbie."

"What do you think will happen?"

"I'd say you have a good shot at a self-defense plea. Samson himself was guilty of . . ."

"No, with Joanna," Rudolph interrupted.

"Forget her, Arthur. She's not worth it."

"You don't know her," he shot back angrily, displaying genuine emotion for the first time since entering the bar.

Joe D. didn't know her well, but he thought he understood her. If Rudolph wasn't already broken he'd tell him that Joanna was like her paintings, easy to read but hard to admire.

"We should head uptown," he said. "And you should call a lawyer."

Rudolph waited a few moments, lost in thought, doubtless of Joanna. Then he stood up abruptly, almost violently. "Let's go," he said. "Let's get this over with."

THIRTY-FIVE

Seymour Franklin told Joe D. he'd send a check, but Joe D. insisted on picking it up himself. He'd spent ten days on the case at $300 each, plus expenses, which were minimal. After putting away a third for taxes, he'd be left with two thousand dollars. Half of that would go toward his share of the monthly mortgage and maintenance payments. That would leave him one thousand dollars until the next assignment rolled in. April was, unfortunately, one of the shortest months, which meant that next month's mortgage and maintenance payments would be due painfully soon. Maybe that's why April's the cruelest month.

Joe D. had called Franklin at his home. A maid had answered and said Mr. Franklin was at his office. At first Joe D. was surprised at how quickly Franklin had gotten a new position. Then the maid gave him the number and Joe D. recognized the exchange right away: Samson Stores.

"With Mona more or less out of commission, I was invited

by the board to resume my responsibilities," Franklin explained on the phone. "I have you to thank for that."

Joe D. let this ride. There was nothing particularly satisfying about the resolution of the case. Samson was dead, for real this time. Arthur Rudolph, Junior, was free on bail, awaiting a trial in which he'd plead self-defense and probably get a suspended sentence; Mona Samson was also free on bail, awaiting trial for conspiracy to commit fraud and murder. Arnot was cooperating with the police and was awaiting sentencing for conspiracy to commit fraud but not murder. Estelle was dead, the true victim in this whole affair, along with the cabdriver. And Seymour Franklin was back in charge of Samson Stores. Somehow Joe D. just didn't feel like celebrating. Franklin said he'd leave a check with his secretary.

Joe D. introduced himself to the receptionist on the executive floor of the Samson Stores Building, and waited a few moments for Franklin's secretary to come get him. You'd never know from the orderly, efficient atmosphere of this place that its founder had just been killed while trying to escape with his male lover to the Caribbean, and his wife and largest shareholder had been indicted for murder. It seemed that Samson had after all created something bigger than himself, something that had a life of its own and would continue to churn out profits with or without him.

Franklin's secretary arrived a few minutes later, an envelope in her hand. She was young and attractive and probably never wore anything sold in Samson Stores, despite the inevitable employee discount. He wondered, briefly, what had happened to Samson's secretary, Felicia Ravensworth. More than likely she was a reminder of the old regime, and had been let go, as they say. "Here you are, Mr. DiGregorio. Mr. Franklin sends his best regards."

Joe D. took the envelope and had the irrational feeling that he was being bought off. The secretary looked at him a moment, expecting a response. When Joe D. realized this he thanked her, and she turned and left.

He put the envelope in his pocket and headed for the elevators. While waiting he decided to open it. What he found surprised him. He'd been paid one week in advance, so he expected a check for the balance due him, fifteen hundred, plus expenses. Instead he found a check for ten thousand dollars.

Joe D. hurried back to the reception area but didn't stop to announce himself this time. Instead he walked straight back to Franklin's office, bypassing his secretary. Franklin was hunched over his big desk, studying a page of dense figures. "This check's for a lot more than you owe me," Joe D. said. He could swear it took a second for his voice to reach the end of the room where Franklin sat.

"A bonus for a job well done."

So it wasn't a mistake. Joe D. didn't know why this made him feel uncomfortable. "I don't feel right taking it," he said. "Samson's dead . . ." Joe D. hesitated. What he was about to say was that a lot of people are just as happy that he is dead, present company included. "Samson's dead and Estelle Ferguson's dead and maybe I could have prevented that." This was the unpleasant idea he couldn't shake since discovering Samson's body on Tuesday.

"Samson was a murderer and a fraud and a . . ." Franklin stopped himself, but Joe D. guessed the next word would refer to his sexuality, which Franklin probably equated with murder and fraud anyway.

"Still . . ."

"Keep it. Or give it to charity, I don't care. A ten thousand dollar bonus is nothing to get too excited about, I can assure you. Do you have any idea, the numbers that are involved in Samson's estate? Hundreds of millions. Your ten thousand is just a footnote to a footnote in the Samson financial statements, rest assured."

This was hardly comforting to Joe D. He shrugged and tried to thank Franklin, but couldn't muster the words.

"We often have need of security services, you know," Franklin said. "I have your number."

"I appreciate that," Joe D. said, and turned to leave.

He felt richer but not happier as he headed back to the elevators. He glanced into the big corner office that had once belonged to George Samson, and was surprised to find it occupied. "Hi there," he said, and again had the sensation of waiting for his voice to reach the other end.

"Good morning," replied Joanna Freeling. She was seated behind her uncle's enormous desk, piles of papers overlapping in front of her. As usual she was wearing black, but this time she had on a black jacket over a white blouse. A suit!

"I never expected to find you here."

"I'm the majority shareholder. Or at least I will be when my aunt is found guilty, which I'm sure she will be. The shares pass to me in the event of her death or incapacity, which apparently includes life imprisonment."

"Are you here permanently?" Joe D. walked halfway toward Joanna's desk and stopped.

Joanna shrugged. "Let's just say indefinitely."

"How do you like the world of big business?"

She leaned back in the big leather chair, which tilted back with her. "It's really fascinating, you know. I feel I can make a difference here. I have a lot of ideas about our merchandising strategy, and I've already been in touch with the advertising agency that handles our account."

Our strategy. *Our* account. How proprietary she'd become. "Have you given up painting?"

"Only for the time being. I have a considerable investment in this company now, and I have to be sure that it's managed properly. It's not about money, you know."

"What's it about, then?"

"Power. Control. Self-reliance."

"Have you been in touch with Arthur?"

He saw a cloud fall over her face, and then he saw it lifted. "No. And I hope I never see him again, ever."

Joe D. couldn't blame her, though he felt sorry for Rudolph. "Anyway, nice to see you. I think this office becomes you." He knew he sounded sarcastic and he didn't care. He turned to leave.

"It's not *about* money, you know," he heard her say behind him.

It never is, he thought to himself as he tucked the check back into his jacket pocket.

Back at the apartment he called Alison at the store, and told her he wanted to celebrate his newfound wealth. The owner of Many Fetes was never one to say no to a celebration. He said he'd pick her up at 6:30.

He changed into shorts and jogged to the reservoir. It was a warm and sunny day, and Central Park looked especially inviting, not at all the murder-and-mayhem preserve of out-of-towners' nightmares. He circled the reservoir three times, propelled by an overwhelming sense of relief. The Samson case was behind him, and ahead lay a future that he thought he could finally begin to envision. It looked OK. He ran a fourth lap, for a total of six-plus miles.

He entered the store at exactly 6:30. Alison was wearing a blouse and slacks. "Where are we going? Should I change?"

He told her it was a surprise, but that she should wear something special. He had put on his only suit. Alison flipped through some dresses, pulling out a few, studying them, and then replacing them. Finally she selected a short black sequined dress, and changed into it in the dressing room. Joe D. caught his breath when she emerged. She looked, literally, breathtaking, the glittery black dress a perfect complement to her pale complexion and lustrous black-brown hair.

"Dressy enough?" she asked, spinning around for him.

"You can't sell that dress, not after tonight. You have to retire it forever."

She checked the price tag dangling from a sleeve. "We could pay for a winter vacation on what I'd make on this dress."

"Forget it. The dress is out of circulation."

The limousine was waiting out front for them when Alison locked up. He helped her lower the heavy metal gates that covered the entire storefront. She looked completely incongruous, wrestling with the gate in that dress.

"I don't believe this," she said as she got in the limo. The driver turned around and said "Okay, sir?" to Joe D., who nodded. They glided up Third Avenue and made a left on Seventy-ninth, heading for the park.

"Where are we going?" Alison asked.

"You'll see. First, let's drink." He opened a bottle of good white wine that was cooling in an ice bucket. He'd considered champagne, but neither he nor Alison was crazy about it, though it always seemed festive to pop the cork. He poured them each a glass.

"Hey, the driver's circling the park again," Alison said, after he poured her a second glass.

"Per my instructions."

"Where are we going to eat, then?"

He leaned forward and picked up a bag from the front seat. "All your favorite things. Moo shu pork. Sauteed green beans. General what's-his-name's chicken."

"So we're just going to drive around the park all night eating take-out?"

He couldn't tell if she was disappointed. "That was the idea. Nice views, not too many traffic lights."

She smiled and moved closer to him and began to sing. " 'Heaven, I'm in heaven. . . .' "

They savored the wine and each other. As the limo sped around Central Park, Joe D. felt as if he were leaving behind everything in his life that had held him back. He was moving into his future, *their* future. He knew, now, that you couldn't wait for the future to slow down for you, and, worse, that you couldn't count on things to work out. You just had to have faith that you'd survive.

"I even brought an appetizer," he said. He reached into the big bag of Chinese food and brought out a small white carton. He handed it to Alison. "Spring rolls?" she said as she opened it. "No, too cold for spring rolls. Noodles?"

She unfolded the cardboard flaps and looked puzzled at first. Then she looked shocked. Then she began to cry. "I love you so much, Joe D.," she said, as tears tumbled down her cheeks.

"Well, try it on," he said. She held out her left hand. "Put it on for me," she said. And he did, as the big car glided smoothly through the gilded park.